CHASING ZERO

BY

W.H. BESWICK

TO CLIVE CUSSLER FOR GIVING US DIRK PITT AND ALL THOSE WONDERFUL ADVENTURES.

A special thanks to Julia Fox for all your hard work and comments. Also, thank you to Adrienne Lawrence for reading the first draft and making suggestions.

PROLOGUE

I am Ellie. You have heard of me, right? If not, what rock have you been hiding under? Bestie to Reggan Sobe. That's right, the girl with the cat eyes. I know you have heard about the other jerks claiming not only that they were her best friends but were there when the world went down the toilet.

Yeah, right. Losers!

I was there. I am the one who never gave up on my best friend, even when the world had turned against her. I had her back. Many bodies are scattered around Oregon to back me up on that fact.

Yeah, that's right. I killed aliens, mutants, and people. Most of those were puppy killers. Can you say that? I don't think so.

Hopefully, you have read Reggan's book, which should have been on the New York Times's best-seller list. I know there is no more New York Times or New York, but that doesn't change the fact that it would have been on it. It would have made her rich if money meant anything now. It would have made a great movie.

If you haven't read it, here is a quick rundown. Earth was all nice and peaceful. Well, not really. We were trying to kill each other for the dumbest reasons. We were polluting the hell of this world. Morons that we were, we just stood around going Dudddde! Don't get me started on politicians. We all know what jerks they turned out to be.

You should know this. Still trying to believe you still need to read Reggan's book.

Okay, the world was pretty screwed up, and the aliens showed up. Bad news: they were total jerks who wanted to take over the world and kill us. Good news: Surprise! There was no good news.

My editor told me I should take that out. Screw her. I am here to tell the truth. If you guys can't handle it, then stop reading. I am the voice in the wilderness. I am the idiot telling you to wake up and not believe all the lies you have heard about the best friend anyone could have.

The big lie. Yes. Reggan is Zero. Yes, she changed. No, she didn't turn into an alien mutant that killed thousands of people. Morons, that is not even possible, even with an MP5 and a very sweet M86 sniper's rifle. I am here to tell you every person and alien Zero killed had it coming, and I am sure that most of my kills were good.

I have a little of an anger management problem, which sometimes results - not always – in me pulling the trigger a little too quickly. That doesn't mean they didn't have it coming.

Before you say, 'That's not what I heard.' Were you there? I don't think so. New Jersey was there. Trisha was there.

Nope, don't remember seeing you there.

Now listen up. I will tell you what happened. You don't want to know the truth?

Stop reading.

Big surprise: my editor, agent, and publisher want me to take out that last sentence.

As if.

CHAPTER 1

I am pissed. You may ask why I am pissed. Because I am sitting in the back of my parent's stupid electric car. Stupid, because when the battery goes dead, we will be walking. They are dragging my ass out of town, leaving my best friend in a coma and dying from an alien disease. So not cool. They are terrified that we might catch it.

News flash, Mom and Dad.

The aliens are here. So, the disease is here. Deal with it. We are all going to die.

They are such hypocrites. Before all the end-of-the-world stuff started, they were vegan. Hardcore vegans. Tried to get rid of my leather boots and jackets. You wouldn't believe what I did to stop that. Totally embarrassed my parents. One the best days of my life. If you haven't figured it out, I am not a vegan. I love meat. I will go as far as to say I have hunted down Bambi's daddy and had him for dinner. Any stag with a ten-point antler comes in my gun sights, and he would have gone down.

My editor just told me that would alienate my readers, as if I cared. I am trying to tell the truth here, and the truth offends a lot of people. Besides, if God didn't want me to eat deer, why did he make them so tasty?

Sorry if I have offended you.

Mom and Dad are eating meat like it's the last days. Duh. It is the last day.

Okay. I got to back up here. You might need a quick history lesson about what is going on.

About two years ago, while we Earthlings were messing up our planet and minding our own business regarding what was happening in the universe, the aliens showed up.

Talk about ugly. No cosmetic surgeon could help these guys, especially with those huge bat-like ears and bug eyes. Not to mention, they all could have used a few hours on the beach or in a tanning booth. Talk about pale. Enough on the visual. You get the idea. They were aliens.

They came here with the whole 'we-are-here-to-help.' We are just some highly advanced aliens who came to Earth to help you over-educated apes.

I will give them this: They actually helped. The aliens brought some really cool stuff to clean up our world. Clean air and clean water are good things. They even got everyone talking about peace and love.

Lies!

A few months after they show up, wars start to break out all over Europe, the Middle East, China, and Russia. The worst kind of war. We are talking about launching those missiles and dropping those bombs that should never have been invented. If this wasn't bad enough, a nasty virus started killing billions.

Bottom line.

In a matter of months, billions are dead, and what was once Europe, China, Russia, and Africa are now nuclear wastelands. We are not talking about Mad Max Wasteland, where everyone is wearing leather and driving totally cool, souped-up cars. We're talking about burning hot ground with air that will kill you in minutes. If that doesn't get you, let's not forget that alien virus I told you about.

Now, ask yourself where the good old U.S.A. was. We were still listening to the advice of our new alien buddies. We sat those wars out. They told us not to worry. They could clean up the radioactive mess and not worry about that virus. And we bought that line. How stupid were we?

In their defense, they did start to clean it up, but only after everyone was dead. Do the math. That meant only the Western Hemisphere was left with humans—maybe some in Africa and definitely most in Australia. Those Aussies never trusted those aliens from day one. It was the only country that said no thanks. Please stay out of our country. For those who failed geography, the Western Hemisphere—that's where we Americans live.

Then, some clever person realized that the aliens had a hand in starting the wars. Needless to say, this pissed us off.

What? The aliens aren't our friends?

A lesson learned too late.

By this time, the aliens had built two strongholds in the middle of America, strategically placed to divide the country into two parts. The war between us and the aliens officially started. We still have our armies and all those wonderful weapons, except for the nuclear weapons that the aliens talked us into destroying.

They wanted a nice, clean war, and I will give them points for that. However, we still had them outnumbered and surrounded.

The aliens decided to even out the playing field by taking out most of our electronics. I'm still trying to figure out how they did that, but I was impressed. Do you get the picture I am painting here? There are no lights, T.V.s, computers, or Internet.

No loss there, in my opinion. Put an end to Facebook and cyberbullying. I do miss texting, only because it was so handy and fast.

The bottom line is that all our fancy super weapons and vehicles are suddenly useless. Older cars, trucks, and motorcycles seemed to survive. I had seen some really old helicopters and jets flying over the city. They probably got them out of mothballs, or the Army had stashed them somewhere just in case.

My parent's electric car is still working for some reason.

For now.

Think that is bad? It got worse when that virus reared its ugly head over here. People started dying here. Not just in the war zones. It spread faster than a juicy piece of gossip about the Kardashians. Everyone was getting sick, and no one lived. You died this horrible death, vomiting and bleeding from every hole. It was truly disgusting.

Three guesses about where the virus came from: Think Cortez, Aztecs, and smallpox. You got it. The aliens brought it with them. Did they know this? Did our ancestors know the blankets they gave the Indians were full of smallpox? The answer is a big yes.

Sorry about the Indian thing. They're Native Americans, not Indians. Come to think of it. I think the P.C. police are gone.

I was living in Cornwall, Oregon when the aliens came. I was there when all hell broke loose. I was right by my friend Reggan when she dropped to the ground and vomited blood. I held her in my arms and hugged while all you losers ran. I rode to the hospital with her. I stayed until my stupid parents came to get me, telling me we were leaving town. I refused to leave. I was kicking some serious ass. Kicking and screaming and was winning until some jerk of a doctor gave me a shot.

BAM!

The next thing I knew, I was waking up in the back of my parents' car and heading out of town.

CHAPTER 2

Being right all the time would be cool. It's not. I know this because my parents and I are walking down the road. As I predicted, the electric car died. Fortunately, we had nothing to carry because my genius parents didn't pack anything. Nothing. No food. No water. No warm jacket. Which is why I am freezing my butt off. At least it is not raining, a rare thing in Oregon this time of the year.

So I could be in a better mood. This explained why I was walking ahead of my parents with my arms wrapped around myself, wishing I had my hunting jacket. Sweet, waterproof material with natural goose down in the lining. I stopped to get my bearings. It was time to stop fuming and start thinking. We were heading East on the 34. How far had we traveled? Not that far. We could be close to Lebanon. That was like 19 miles from Cornwall. We could almost be there. If I got my parents to Lebanon, they would be safe. Then I go back to Cornwall. Even if I don't get a ride, I could hike that no problem. I could be back by Reggan's bed in two, three days tops.

I had a plan.

I turned to Mom and Dad and gave them my best smile. "I figure we are real close to Lebanon. Isn't that where Aunt May lives?"

"Yes, that was where we were heading," Mom said, looking tired. Dad didn't look any better. They were both accountants, not big on the outdoors. Order was their God. Everything is in its place and a place for everything. Looking at them, I realized that this new world probably terrified them. I could see the fear in their eyes. They really wanted their old world back. Suddenly, I felt bad for them. They were my parents. Sure, they did some stupid stuff. What parent didn't? Although the vegan thing was a pain in the butt, I still loved them. The world they loved and felt safe in was gone. Chances are it would probably never return. That thought made me realize I better start stepping up, or me and my parents would be screwed.

I gave them my best smile and walked up to Mom. I gave her a hug and another smile. "We can do this. Let me help you. We will be fine. Aunt May makes great fried chicken. You guys are going to love it."

So, I helped my parents with words of encouragement. I even found some water and apples in an abandoned house. No jackets, just some oversized, hideous sweaters. Left behind for obvious reasons. Mom and Dad were feeling pretty good. So was I.

Then, the Army truck pulled up.

CHAPTER 3

Fortunately, we didn't have to ride in the back of the truck for very long. It was just us, another family of four, and two soldiers in full gear. They were holding M16s. I had heard the Army was switching over to M4s. I guess these guys didn't rate the upgrade, or maybe the war changed everything. Right now, I wouldn't say no to an M16. MP5 would be sweet but those were hard to come by.

The truck moved along a bumpy road. I could hear the sounds of trucks and maybe helicopters. Muffled voices yelling stuff. The truck came to a stop. The soldiers jumped out and asked us to follow them.

I climbed out. It was night, but there were bright lights all around, so I took a moment to take everything in. It turned out the bright lights were coming from spotlights scanning the ground. I stared at the long huts made of wood with tin roofs. Then, I took in the towers with guards armed with 50-caliber machine guns. We were surrounded by a high barbed wire fence, with more guards patrolling the outside.

A captain in green fatigues with a big smile walked up and nodded to everyone. "Welcome to Camp Beaver. You have been moved here for your own safety. First, I will give you your hut assignments. After you get settled, we'll get you some hot food and showers. Sound good?"

Everyone was thrilled.

I looked around the camp and knew what it was. I had seen THE GREAT ESCAPE.

This was a prison camp.

CHAPTER 4

I used to like pasta, especially with a nice thick sauce with red meat. My friend Reggan can make the best spaghetti with venison. To die for. The pasta here is almost every day and is usually under or overcooked, served with a red or yellow sauce that tasted so bad you prayed for the canned crap.

Disgusting.

Served with salads made with lettuce that was more brown than green and stale white bread.

Yuck.

It has been at least two weeks. There really wasn't anything to do. Some kids had been playing baseball until our keepers took away the bats.

My guess is they were afraid they could be used as weapons. The worst part was there was nothing to do or read. I could feel my brain cells dying. We only saw Mr. Happy Face Captain when new people were brought in. Then, he would leave very quickly. Most of the soldiers stayed outside the wire and just watched us. Three times a day, a sergeant came with a tall, skinny private with a clipboard and did a head count. If anyone was missing, they went looking for the person. They were usually dead or dying, but not always from the virus. Some people had killed themselves.

Very sad. Fear is not always a good thing.

For the record, I noticed new soldiers kept popping up. Where did the old ones go? I had a pretty good idea the virus was not just behind the wire.

I spent most days wandering around the compound close to the wire. Yes. I was plotting my escape. Tunneling was out. So the way to freedom was through the wire, past the guards, and then into the nearby woods. The guards were no problem. They spent most of their time talking to each other and not watching the camp. At night, only tower guards clicked their spotlights on and off throughout the night. Every thirty minutes, they swept the camp for about two minutes. The spotlights went off, and they went back to being bored. The wire was the problem. I needed something to cut my way out. Just on the other side of the fence was a green shack made of wood. I had spotted the soldiers taking tools out from this shack. I knew there would be some wire cutters inside.

Of course, if I could get to the shack, I wouldn't need the wire cutters.

I told myself there had to be a way out. I needed to think outside the box. The prisoners in THE GREAT ESCAPE made their own tools, but I am not some genius POW. When I wasn't standing close to plotting my escape, I was working out—pushups, pullups, and running laps around the camp. I saw a lot of running in my future.

One day, while I was chilling by the fence after my thirty laps, the young soldier with the clipboard walked up. It was a little taller than me. Actually, everyone was taller than me. I barely made it past five feet. I have long blond hair, blue eyes, and a few freckles. Reggan tells me I am really cute. I keep having to tell her that she is a total babe. The girl doesn't believe me. She had self-image issues. What seventeen-year-old doesn't? Me. I am perfectly comfortable with who I am and how I look. My only major character flaw is I have a short temper and even shorter patience with losers and jerks. Sadly, the world is filled with them. Which could explain the short temper.

"They know you are thinking of trying to escape," the soldier said with a smile. "They make jokes about it."

"Do they?" I said, turning and looking at the skinny guy. His green fatigues seemed too big for him. He had black hair and a slim face with a spattering of dark freckles. His smile was filled with crooked teeth, but it worked for him. I couldn't help but notice he didn't have a weapon. "Let me guess. Dumb blonde jokes or stupid kid jokes?"

"Both. They laugh it off. They don't think you are a threat," he said with another smile. "I think they're underestimating you. I think you are going to get out of here. I think you just figured it out."

"Do tell," I said, suddenly feeling very nervous. I had been studying the fence. It hit me. The bottom piece of barbed wire was about four or five inches off the ground. It rained last night, so the ground was muddy. Soft. I could burrow under the wire in no time. It was supposed to rain again tonight. Perfect cover. The guards would be more interested in keeping dry than keeping their eyes on the fence. I noticed the soldier had a thick accent. What was it? "Where you from, soldier?"

"New Jersey. I am not even supposed to be here," the soldier said. "I barely made it through basic. They only kept me because I have a gift."

"That would be?"

"I'm a computer whiz."

"Computers don't work anymore."

"No. No. Computers would work fine if they were turned off during the big blackout. Sure, the Internet and almost all forms of electronic communication are gone. The laptops and desktops still work. The bitch is keeping the batteries powered up. All the power plants are down. You just can't plug into the wall anymore. Thank God you guys in Oregon thought using solar panels was a great idea. You can't see them, but several solar panels are outside the camp. We use the computers to store files and other stuff."

"Like doing a body count?" I said, turning to him. You count the bodies and add them up on your still-working computer. Keep a record of how long it takes the virus to become contagious and then how long it takes people to die.

"See? I knew you were smart. Probably pretty tough. You probably know your way around a gun. I've seen how you check out the weapons the soldiers are carrying. I bet you could identify and use every weapon in this place."

"I am probably a better shot than you."

"Who isn't? Remember, I barely got through basic," he said with a laugh. "That's why I don't have a gun."

"How does a computer nerd end up in the army?" I asked. "Shouldn't you be at MIT or something?"

"I come from the poor section of New Jersey. I'm very good with computers. Can even write some decent programs. But I am not gifted like those hackers you hear about. I needed money for college. If I serve four years, the Army pays my way through. Everything was going according to plan, but then the aliens showed up."

"They screwed everyone, not just you," I said. "You got a name, soldier?"

"New Jersey."

"That's where you're from?" I said with a snort. I was still debating whether I liked this guy. I didn't trust him, but that didn't mean I couldn't like him. He was nice in a pathetic way. "What's your real name?"

"Elwood," he muttered, looking around. "Elwood Blue."

"Like the..."

"Yeah, yeah, like the character from that T.V. show and movie. My parents were big fans," Elwood said. "Parents don't even think about the ramifications of the names they give their kids. At the time, they thought it was so cool. Like that couple on T.V. who named their kid Saint? Trust me. He is going to get nothing but grief with that name. I have heard every joke about sunglasses, black suits, and why can't I sing."

"Dude. Issues much?"

"Look. I was stationed in Washington, but they sent me here a few weeks ago. All the soldiers have heard the rumors about some girl surviving the virus."

"No one survives."

"This girl did. She caught it. Almost died. Then, I woke up. They are all excited about the possibility of a cure. You know what that would mean?"

"We could win the war," I said, thinking this was a game changer.

"I was sent here because it is true," New Jersey said, looking serious. "Not only did this girl in Cornwall survive. Some doctors actually came up with a cure. He was so excited he got some local companies to start churning it out. This really pissed off the guys in Washington."

"Why?" I asked. I think I have made my position clear on what I think of guys back in Washington. If I haven't, I think they are all jerks who will do anything to keep their jobs, and I do mean anything.

"I haven't figured that out yet," he said, moving closer and looking around. "I do know they tried to stop the drug from being made, but it was already on the trucks being delivered all over the country. I am telling you this because you may want to stick around. Soldiers, including the brass, are dying too. Someone has started the rumor that the cure is here, and the colonel is keeping it locked up."

"Unhappy soldiers with guns is not a good thing for a commanding officer," I said, moving closer. "I can wait, but not too long."

"Trust me. One, two days tops," New Jersey said, starting to walk away.

"New Jersey," I called out as he walked away. "You said the girl lived in Cornwall? I don't suppose you know her name?"

"You think you might know her?"

"Cornwall is a very small town. The biggest thing there is the university."

"Oh yeah. Fighting Otters. I heard someone say it. Something funny about her last name sounding like a drink."

"Reggan Sobe?" I asked, walking up to him and grabbing his arm.

"Yeah, that's it. You know her?"

"My best friend," I said, realizing Reggan had beaten the odds. She was alive. My best friend was alive. Now, I had another reason to escape—the best reason in the world—I was going to find my friend.

CHAPTER 5

Funny thing about God. He seems to like to screw with you. Just when things are going great. He throws you a curveball. This curve ball hit me right in the face. I was walking back to my hut when it hit me.

Pain. Dizziness. I dropped to my knees and vomited. As I collapsed, I thought, 'screw you, God.' Another reason I am agnostic. Not an atheist. They seem a little too angry for my taste. Besides, I refuse to believe the human race happened by sheer accident.

I don't know how long I was out. I faded in and out. When I was awake, I was throwing up. Someone was constantly wiping the blood from my face. I'll tell you this; I wanted to die. I really did. This was pain like I never knew.

Then suddenly, I was awake and feeling pretty good, not great. I couldn't get out of bed because I was so weak and hungry. I would have welcomed that crappy pasta and old salad. All I was getting was tasteless thin soup, that fake orange drink, and the astronaut's drink and water. Lots of water.

When I felt better, I hoped New Jersey would come by. He didn't. I did pick up that my collapsing in the camp sparked the revolt. The colonel had been forced to give out the drug. The drug that had saved my life. I figured on another day, I would look for New Jersey myself.

Once again. Best laid plans.

I was kind of napping on my cot when three soldiers in black with a doctor walked up to me. They studied me. The doctor looked nervous. "This one you want."

"You're Ellie, right?" The biggest soldier asked.

"Who wants to know?" I snapped, deciding I didn't like these guys.

"That's her," the soldier said with a smile and nod. "I heard she had an attitude. Ellie, we are moving you and your parents to a more secure location."

"Why?"

"I can't go into detail, but everything has changed. It is a whole new war now. Your friend Reggan Sobe is the reason."

The next thing I know, I am lying on a stretcher with only that fashionable hospital robe and blanket to keep me warm. I was carried out to a truck where my parents were waiting. It was a short ride to wherever they were taking me. I looked around. It was another camp, but different. There were long U-shaped huts made of corrugated tin, along with tents. In the middle was a three-store building that could have been an office building once. This was where they took me and dumped me in a small room with a cot and nothing else. Mom and Dad said they would be right back, so I was left alone with my thoughts. At least I was warm. Still weak, I just laid there for a while drifting in and out sleep. I heard voices coming from the hallway and outside when I was awake. I couldn't make out the words, but there was a lot of yelling.

And the occasional gunshot. Not a series of gunshots. Just one every now and then. In my mind, this wasn't a good thing.

I was finally able to sit up and walk around without feeling dizzy. Suddenly, I was famished. I pulled on the door knob.

Locked.

Never a good sign.

CHAPTER 6

So, I was a prisoner. It had to be because I was best friends with Reggan. I couldn't figure out what was going on. What had Reggan done to piss off the Army? She survived the virus. She had let them use her blood to create a cure. For some reason, the Army held back the cure.

Once again, for those with short-term memories. I am not a big fan of the government. I consider all politicians liars. Even if the president of the United States told me it was raining outside, I would still look out the window and wouldn't be surprised to find it was sunny. I mean, look at the state of our country. The world? Do these guys look like they are working for you? I know who the politicians work for, and they live on Wall Street. The UFO that crashed years ago at Roswell has something to do with this. I watched the X files. That show had a lot more truth to it than any other show on T.V.

Sorry, I'm getting off track. Bottom line here. I am pretty sure these soldiers and the government are up to no good. I have read books where powerful people take advantage during a war to increase their power or just save their own butts. So, from this point on, I don't trust anybody, including my mom and dad. They are just too scared to be trusted. My plan is to get out of here and find Reggan. She obviously needs me to watch her back.

Just as I was making this decision, the door opened. Speak of the devil. Mom and Dad walked in with big smiles on their faces. Mom was holding a tray with glass milk, water, and the sorriest-looking burger and fries I had ever seen.

They looked delicious.

"Thanks, Ma, I'm starving," I said, taking the tray and putting it on my cot. I gave her a hug and smile, then gulped down the milk. I took a bite of the burger. It tasted better than it looked. "So what's going on? Why am I locked in this room?"

"Oh honey, it is for your own protection," Mom said, sitting on the bed beside me. "Reggan has gotten herself into some trouble. Terrible trouble."

"Reggan? Mom, Reggan is the nicest, sweetest person I know. She is incapable of being bad. It's just not in her genes," I said, wolfing down the burger as I talked. The fries were soggy, and there was no ketchup. I ate them anyway. "This is a huge mistake."

"We just talked to the general, and he says otherwise," Dad said, folding his arms across his chest. "Apparently, the disease changed Reggan. I know this is hard to believe, but she killed some soldiers."

"If Reggan killed some soldiers, they had it coming. Mom. Dad. Reggan couldn't even shoot a deer. No way could she shoot a human. Something is wrong here."

"Listen, Ellie, you have to help them," Mom said, touching my arm. "Reggan escaped. We both know you would know where she would run off to. That bunker her grandfather made back in the hills."

"I don't know where that is," I lied, trying to look as innocent as possible. As I was thinking this, I realized that Reggan might go to another place, but I didn't think she knew about the sporting goods store in Mammoth.

Mammoth was a tiny town about twenty-eight miles from Cornwall. I really needed to get out of here. Lying again. "You know Reggan's grandad was crazy."

"Don't lie to us," Dad snapped. "You liked that crazy old fool. I saw you talking to him plenty of times."

"Crazy people are fun to talk to," I said with a smile. "A lot of people seem to think I am a little crazy."

"Ellie! This is not a game," Dad snarled. "You will help them find Reggan. It's our ticket out of here."

"You help them, and they will fly us down to Texas," my mom said, pulling me closer and hugging me. "Things are safer down there."

"No surprise there. You got Texans and guns. I wouldn't be surprised to find there wasn't one alien alive in the whole state." I said with a shake of my head. "Why don't you just go to Texas? I'm staying here."

"Ellie, how are we supposed to get to Texas?" Dad said, looking down at me with genuine anger in his face. Or was that fear? "The country is divided in half. We'll never make it on foot. The only way to get there is by plane."

"I bet I could get there on foot," I said, finishing the fries. I sipped some of the water. "Look, I can't go to Texas. It is obvious that Reggan needs me."

"So help the Army find her. They are not going to kill her," Mom said. "But you are not understanding the problem. Reggan is no longer the Reggan you knew. She is different. If you find her, she will kill you."

"No, she wouldn't," I growled, suddenly angry. I glared at my parents. "I am not going to sell out my best friend so you can get a couple airplane tickets."

"Why are you always like this? This not about some stupid leather boots!" Dad yelled. "This is about our lives. Will you do the right thing for once in your life? We are family. Families stick together during times like these. Tell them what they want to know."

I still couldn't believe Reggan had turned into some kind of monster. There was something else going on here. I could feel it in my gut. Reggan had lived when everyone else died. That wasn't supposed to happen. Her surviving the virus screwed up the aliens' plan. They held back the cure as long as possible. Someone else's plan had been screwed up. I looked at my parents and sighed. "I will think about it. I'm tired. Let me sleep."

They hugged me, but I couldn't feel any love. I lay back on the cot and looked up at the ceiling. As I debated what to do, I came up with a plan of escape. A smile spread across my face.

CHAPTER 7

I was just debating on what to do when the door flew open. Two soldiers came, holding M-16s. They stayed by the door. A second later, a guy in an Army dress uniform walked in like he owned the place. There were a lot of ribbons and medals on his chest. Too many. He almost looked like that picture of General Patton from World War 2. Patton pulled the look off. He was a class act. This guy didn't. He was too good-looking and tanned. His smile was too white and quick. The blue eyes were bright but cold. He was holding a chair in one hand. He twirled around so the back was facing me. He straddled the chair, folding his arms over the back, and leaned forward. "Ellie. I am General Watershaw. I am the top guy in this sector now. No more mayor. No more governor. There is just me with a whole army to back me up. No one leaves Oregon and parts of Washington unless I say so."

"So what? Am I supposed to be impressed? I'm not," I said, trying to sound tough, but with my butt sticking out of the hospital gown, it wasn't really working. "I will tell you the same thing that I told my parents. I don't know where Reggan is or where she would go. She is an okay tracker but not really the outdoorsy type. Now, me? You give me a gun, warm clothes, and a head start, and you are never going to find me."

"You're seventeen, right?" Watershaw said with another smile. "I can see you were not taught to respect your elders."

"I respect my friends and my betters," I said, pushing back my long hair. I was studying the chair. It was a lovely wood straight back. Just what I needed. "I just don't understand what all the fuss is about. Do you actually want me to believe my best friend has turned into some kind of monster? I don't think so. There is something else going on."

"What part of your friend being infected by an alien virus don't you get? It changed her. Reggan Sobe is no longer the person you knew," he said, resting his chin on his hands. "I am like you. I don't like games. I am impatient. I need answers now. So I have gotten permission from your parents to use truth serum."

"Sodium Pentothal?" I smirked. "That only works in the movies."

"I got something much better in mind. It will be here in the morning." The general said. "Remember, this isn't the movies. Where is the bunker?"

"Not a clue."

"All right, girlie, have it your way," Watershaw said. He got up and left. The soldiers followed him out and closed the door. I heard the lock click.

"Screw you!" I said, jumping up and grabbing the chair. I put it on top of my cot. Then, I climbed onto the chair. My head bumped against the ceiling tile, pushing it up. I used my hands to push it up and looked around the open area above the tiles. Who says you can't learn something from T.V.? I glanced back down at the door and then pulled myself up.

CHAPTER 8

I was now balancing on one of the support beams. I used my hands and feet to move along the narrow piece of wood. A noise below would make me freeze, so I stood in place until I felt it was safe to move again. I could hear muffled voices but no yelling. I took this as a good sign. No one had noticed my escape.

Yet.

Every so often, I would stop and carefully lift a tile, checking out the room below. So far, there had been nothing but offices. I was about to give up when I lifted a tile and stared at a shelf filled with green shirts. I carefully climbed down into the room and looked around.

It was a huge room filled with new metal racks containing Army gear. Everything I needed was here.—well, not everything. There were no guns.

I needed a gun.

Thinking about that made me think of an old cartoon with the rabbit who thinks he is an Army sergeant and yells at the dumb hunter, "Why does every other man in the army have a rifle, and you have a gun?"

I moved up and down the aisles, taking what I needed. I would stop to make a quick size check. Almost everyone is taller than me, but it turned out the Army was taking short guys. I found some camouflage fatigues that fit along with some thermal underwear. Socks and boots that were a little big but worked until I found some others. I found a thick jacket with a hood and cap. Now fully clothed, I searched and found a backpack. This was filled with more socks and another set of thermals. Finally, I packed some MRE rations because there was nothing else to eat.

Note to self: Only eat if you are starving. Remember, Reggan's Granddad let me try one. It was gross, and I spent too much time in the bathroom afterward.

There were no weapons of any kind, not even knives. No other gear like a compass or binoculars. I pulled on some gloves and went to the back. Through a window, I watched the now-dark camp. It was empty, except for the few guards patrolling outside the barbwire fence. There were towers, but these guys were not watching for me. They were more interested in what was going on outside the wire fence.

I found a back door and slipped out into the night. I pulled up my hood and wandered toward the gate. There were a couple of trucks parked at the front of the building. They looked old, like something used back in World War 2. A big green thing with a canvas covering the back. I watched the drivers leaning against the hood. Both looked bored and were smoking. They were more interested in the ground than anything else. They both shivered.

It was then that I noticed how cold it was. With my luck, it would start to rain. It rains in Oregon a lot.

"Why are you assholes still here?"

I looked up and stared at the small, chubby man with a bulldog-like face. He had sergeant strips on his shoulder. "You are supposed to be halfway to Cornwall by now!"

"Captain Sims told us to wait."

"General Watershaw wants that shipment there by morning. I suggest you get your butts moving!"

The soldiers muttered something and put out their cigarettes. I watched them climb into the truck. The sergeant walked away without looking back. I ran up to the back of the truck as it pulled away. I grabbed the tailgate, pulled up, and managed to roll into the truck. I banged into some crates and boxes. There was just enough room to sit on the floor. I was tempted to look through the boxes, but the truck stopped. There was an exchange of bored voices. I waited. The corner of the tarp was pulled back, making me scrunch down. A face peeked in, and then it was gone.

Lucky me. A moron is protecting the base.

I didn't move until the truck started to move. Only then did I pull out my flashlight and scan the cargo. Most of it was ammo, which was useless to me without a gun. More rations.

No, thank you.

I settled back for what I figured would be a short ride home. Surprisingly, I wasn't tired. I was feeling good when the distant sound of sirens filled the air. I lifted the flap and saw we were only a few miles from the camp. Even from this distance, I could see the whole place lit up. Soldiers were running around. The truck stopped.

I had a bad feeling about this.

I heard the door open, so I climbed up onto the tailgate. Then, I pulled myself up onto the top of the truck. I lay flat and then cursed. My pack was still inside the truck. There was nothing I could do but lie there.

"They checked the back before we left," one of the soldiers said. "I am freezing my butt out here."

"I told them that, but they said to recheck it," another one said, then sneezed. "Geez, it's freezing."

"Yeah, tell me about it. Does it snow here?"

"How the hell would I know?"

I listened as the back flap was pulled back. As I listened, a little rain started to fall.

"What are we looking for? Oh crap, it's raining."

"Chill, it's just drizzling. Some blonde kid escaped. The general wants her back."

"You ask me, Watershaw is crazy and not in a funny or good way. Look, you see a kid?"

"Nope. Okay, now it's raining. Let's radio them and get going."

"I didn't join the Army for this crap. I'm supposed to be out in less than a year. Back at college."

"Bad news. You are not getting out any time soon, and your college has probably been blown to bits."

"Thanks for that pep talk. Can we get back in the truck now?"

I listened to them climb back into the truck, thinking these guys sounded like a couple of old women. As I lay waiting, the rain slowly turned to small flakes. Then the flakes got bigger. When the truck finally started moving, the snow was coming down hard and fast. As I crawled to the back of the truck, I thought it never snowed like this in Oregon. I looked over the back of the truck and watched the ground zip by. It was going to be harder getting back into the truck. The falling snow added to the fun. I got onto my belly and slowly slid back. I got my legs over and carefully moved my lower body over the edge. The bumping around wasn't helping as I used my boots to feel around for the tailgate.

Being short sometimes sucks.

The truck hit another bump. I lost my grip and fell back. I managed to snag the flapping tarp. My body slammed against the back of the truck. My feet were almost touching the ground. The tires were throwing snow and ice against my legs.

It hurt.

I flapped around, hearing the tarp begin to rip. Totally scared, I frantically grabbed for the tailgate. After a few tries, my gloved hand caught it. I let go of the tarp and grabbed the back with both hands. The tips of my boots were being dragged along the road. I cursed as my pants were soaked by the sleet. My first attempt to climb in almost resulted in me falling. On the next try, I managed to pull myself up a little. Then, I used the bumper to push up. Once again, I rolled into the back of the truck. Exhausted, cold, wet, and grateful, I lay on the floor, thankful to be alive.

CHAPTER 9

I was napping when the truck hit another bump. I sat up and looked around, forgetting where I was. There was the sound of muffled voices. That came and went. I lifted the flap and saw we were back in Cornwall. It was time to get out. I pulled on my pack and looked out. The streets were now almost unrecognizable because of the snow covering everything. We had snow before in Cornwall, but not like this. It looked like a scene from that movie where the world is thrown back into another Ice Age.

For the record, I never saw this coming. Not the aliens. I never trusted them from day one. The snow and stuff. That was a real surprise.

I waited for the truck to slow. It finally slowed down enough when the truck was making a turn. I jumped out, landing on my feet. Not bad for a girl who ditched the gym whenever possible.

I stood there and took in my hometown, now covered with snow and ice. Cars buried under the snow sat in the middle of the street. Because of the high snow drifts in front of all the buildings, it took me a second to realize I was in downtown Cornwall. Behind the mounds of snow, I could see broken windows. It looked like some places had been burned out.

A friendly reminder the world I knew was gone, except for the crazy people. Reggan and I might be the only sane people left in the world.

Paranoid much? I don't think so.

I wondered just how many people were left in the world. They had been dropping bombs all over Europe and Russia. The nasty bombs keep killing even after they have exploded. Then the virus came. Another gift from the aliens that we could have done without.

I needed a gun.

Now I know what you are thinking. You said you were a hunter. Don't you have guns at home? No. I do own an excellent Remington

700 and Winchester shotgun, but my parents were vegans and wouldn't let me keep them in the house. I stored them at Reggan's Granddad's house. If they were still there. Which I doubted. They would be in the gun locker in his basement. I didn't have the combination for that. The odds are everything was up at his bunker.

Oh yeah. Reggan's Granddad was a prepper. You know, one of those guys who built underground bunkers and warned everyone the end of the world was coming. People used to laugh at them. Not me. I am no dummy. I read all about Area 51. The Roswell cover-up. I am not some nut. I'm pretty sure that we landed on the moon. Mythbusters pretty much shot down that theory for good. The whole our world leaders are lizards? Not buying that. The government and big business are out to get us? I am a big believer in that. Even before the Kapteyians showed up, we were screwing up the planet. For the record, how dumb are we? We send space probes into the universe containing a map of our planet. Hey, evil aliens! The dumb Earthlings are right here. Come get us. I would not be surprised to find out how the Kapteyians found us.

The guy in his wheelchair had it right. I bet my last dollar he was the only guy besides me who thought that the aliens showing up was a bad thing. I am sorry he died. He was very cool.

My editor pointed out that the reader might need to learn who the Kapteyians are. They are the aliens trying to kill us. They came from a system called Kapteyn. That's the closest place that may have planets that can support life—life as we know it. It is a mere 12.7 lightyears away. Please tell me you know what a light year is.

Okay, for those who don't watch Star Trek or pay attention in science class, a light year is the distance it takes light to travel in a year. The bottom line is that wherever the aliens came from, it wasn't the moon or Mars. They didn't come in a spaceship that had a warp drive. My guess is they used a black hole or something else. I am not going into the folding space theories.

Read a book. Well, I guess you are. My bad.

Okay, the odds are my guns are not at Reggan's Granddad's. They're probably in his bunker. I know where it is, but I don't want to go hiking up into the mountains. For one, the clothes I am wearing aren't waterproof or warm. I am freezing my butt off here.

So where to go?

I decided the best place to start looking for Regina was her house. My friend would go there unless she was with her grandfather. Then, there were three places she would go: home, the bunker, and Mammoth.

Make that four.

Texas was definitely an option. Jersey did say the Texans were kicking butt down there. I still think the open carry law was stupid. If you need to walk around with a gun on your hip, you have issues.

The problem was I didn't know if she was with her parents or Granddad. Her mom and dad didn't get along with Granddad. Could that have changed? Maybe. The best bet is Reggan's house. It was a starting point. I trudged off toward her street, realizing this army boots sucked. My toes were freezing. I occasionally stopped to check a store with something I could use.

Like a gun.

I was heading toward Reggan's house when it hit me. There were clothes at my house—nice, warm clothes that would keep me toasty, warm, and dry. I had a change of plan. I would go to my house. I turned and headed over to my place. This brought me past my old high school. I had to stop to take it all in. It should be no big surprise that I was not a fan of school. One of my best friends loved school.

Not Reggan. Trisha.

Trisha is nothing like me. She is a real fashionista. Her clothes and hair are always perfect. On top of that, she was a cheerleader in the student government. She was every parent's dream kid. So why was she friends with me? We bonded in grade school. She wasn't as much of a pain then, but now I knew she would have my back. Trisha, there may be a lot of things I don't like, but I couldn't ask for a better friend. She puts up with my crap. Next to Reggan, she is my best friend. I could have taken my GED to get out, but I stayed because Reggan stayed. You see, Reggan is almost a genius. She makes jokes about having an almost gifted mind. They gave her the option to just move right into college. She refused. My best friend has self-esteem issues. She is this tall, beautiful girl with the most amazing hair. If Reggan could just get past being taller than most guys in school. She thinks that is the reason she doesn't get dates. Height has nothing to do with this. It is this vibe she puts out. Trisha always offers to give her a makeover. I am totally on board with that. Regina needs to have her self-image boosted. A makeover might do the job.

You tell Trisha that, and I will hunt you down.

I was standing there when I noticed a jeep parked in front of the school. I knew this jeep. How many really old Army jeeps do you see running around Cornwall? I ran over to it and brushed off the snow. It was Reggan's Grandad's jeep.

Why was it here? Reggan's Granddad had come here. Why? The school had been closed weeks ago. I had to take a look inside. They could be hiding out in the school.

I trudged to the locked front door and used the only key I could find—a rock. I had always wanted to do this, but it was less satisfying today. I went through the broken glass door and stepped into a very dark place.

CHAPTER 10

I stood there for a while, letting my eyes adjust to a dark hallway. Then I remembered the flashlight in my pack. Duh. The place not only seemed empty but spooky. A chill ran down my back. I wasn't sure if it was from the cold or just me being a little scared. I took in the wide foyer that should have been crowded with students. Ghosts of a world long since passed.

Finally, I took a deep breath and moved deeper into the building. If you still need to figure it out, Cornwall is a small college town. So the high school is a little small. It's composed of three buildings, but I was sure that they would be in the main building if Reggan and her family were here. I moved slowly, using the flashlight to find my way. The small light beam flickered around the floor and walls. I came to a glass case filled with trophies and pictures. For some reason, I stopped to look at the display. It was for the girls' basketball team. A glint of red caught my eye. I focused the light on one picture. Was Reggan in her uniform with her famous give me a break look and all that red hair.

She hated her hair.

Me and Trisha were in the picture, too. She had just won the game, and we were celebrating. Trisha was hugging her, and I was on the other side doing the famous two fingers over her head joke.

I am such a joker.

A big sadness swept through my body. No, I didn't cry. I am tougher than I look. It was the cold that made my eyes water. I smashed the glass before I realized it. Luckily, I was wearing gloves. I took the picture and stared at it.

God, we looked so happy.

We went out for pizza to celebrate. Then we slept over at Reggan's house. It was a good night. One of the best nights. We had no idea that those nights would soon be gone. I slumped against the wall and slid down to the floor. Then I just sat there for the longest time. The reality of what the world had become and what I was planning on doing finally hit me. I felt so small. I pulled off my cap and ran my fingers through my hair.

Yeah, I cried. Happy?

I don't know how long I sat there, but the footsteps coming from the front of the building brought me back to reality.

CHAPTER 11

I carefully put the picture in my pack and crept down the hall. I peeked around the corner and gasped.

I had only seen the aliens on T.V., in magazines, and on my computer. Seeing them up close and personal...Wow. These guys were definitely not from around here. There were ten, maybe twelve of them. Except for one, they were a lot taller than I thought they would be. He couldn't be much taller than me. They all had the same pale skin and those big bug eyes. You know the kind. Round and bugling out with red veins. Then there were the big web ears adding to the creepy factor. The tall ones were well-muscled, wearing blue jumpsuits with metal plates on their chest and backs. The small one wore a black jumpsuit with the same plate on his chest. They all wore the same silver helmet with openings for their ears. I noted the weapons were all silver with blinking green lights running along the barrels, except for the small guy. He was holding a short, stocky thing. It had a series of gold tubes running from the grip to a cone-shaped barrel with tiny prods mounted. There was a large blinking green light on one side. He turned to the others, talking in the chirps and squeaks that had become so famous. One of the big ones pushed the weapon away from the group. This was followed by the big one yelling at the small one and pointing at the gun.

Something dropped to the floor with a loud crash somewhere in the building. This stopped the arguing and made the aliens look toward me.

Time to go.

I jumped up and ran down the hallway, skidding around a corner, almost falling on my butt because of the melted snow on my boots. I managed to keep on my feet and kept running. The back doors were just around another corner. I could hear the sounds of heavy boots coming up behind me. I made the turn and then stopped.

Snow was piled up against the doors. I couldn't even see out the glass. Had a new ice age started, and no one told me? We get rain. Not this kind of snow. The running feet were coming closer.

I needed a gun.

I looked over at the stairs leading to the second floor. This produced a groan. Every horror movie had the dumb girl running up the stairs to escape whatever monster or masked killer was chasing her. Big surprise. It never ended well for her. I always screamed don't go upstairs. They never listened.

Yes, I ran up the stairs.

What choice did I have?

I charged up to the second floor, trying to remember the layout. I didn't hear any footsteps behind me. Just loud aliens yelling. It sounded like they were cursing. Did aliens curse? They never did in the movies. Most were just being so logical and not showing emotions. Don't get me started on the whole Vulcan and Spock thing. I never bought the 'we have no emotion's thing.' They had emotions. They just spent centuries suppressing them. Which makes them the most frustrated race in the universe. I always figured their sex had to be the most boring in the universe, too. How good can logical sex be?

Boring!

It is a major miracle that race didn't die out from being so dull.

I ran down the hallway, thinking I had to get out of this building. I needed a distraction since I didn't have a gun. I slowed down and started to think.

About time, Ellie.

I stopped when I saw the door for the audio/visual room. This was where the geeks hung out. There was even an ancient reel-to-reel projector inside. There was also the school P.A. system. This was where the cheerleaders, school president, and other self-important morons made announcements. I was thinking of those big alien ears.

Am I a genius or what?

The gods were with me because the door was open. I stepped into the small and cramped room, which was filled with all kinds of junk: computers, laptops, and desktops—all kinds of electric stuff that looked like junk to me. I moved past these and came to the desk where the P.A. system was set. I smiled and then thought, stupid.

No power.

I kicked several things and then glared at the control panel. Then I noticed the small flickering green light.

Power? How? No time to think about it.

I sat down and turned on the mike, turning the volume to loud. I licked my lips and said, "Hello, alien bad guys."

I could hear my voice booming through the hallway outside.

Yes!

Now I need music. Something loud and annoying. I began to look through drawers, looking for C.D.s. There had to be C.D.s because a CD player was built into the console. In the bottom drawer, I scored. There was a stack of C.D.s. I started to go through them, tossing down the rejects. "Crap. Crap. Crap. Crap. Seriously? Mel Torme's greatest hits? Who is the hell was Mel Torme? Whoa. Taylor Swift."

Don't judge. She is one of the best songwriters and singers on the planet. Did you see that badass music video with the guns and leather? That was totally hot. I pushed this into my pack and made a note to find a CD player. Good luck with that. When the world was sane, only old people listened to C.D.s. The last CD turned out to be a winner. It was one of my favorite movies, and it was a musical.

Totally cool.

I put the CD on and pressed play. I peeked out the door and ran back to the stairwell. I waited. Then the music started. The famous guitar strumming. Then, an ever so creepy voice. Then the female singer came in. Just as creepy. The music built up. Moving toward the amazing chorus. The words filled the hallways.

TIME WARP from ROCKY HORROR PICTURE SHOW. Watch it. It will change your life.

The hallways filled with pounding music. I heard boots coming up. I looked around and dragged a table filled with flyers to the staircase. With great skill, I got it balanced over the top step. The aliens came up. One push and bam. It didn't kill them, but hopefully, it caused some pain. I ran down to the other end of the hallway. Red laser beams began to zoom around me. I almost looked back, thinking, where did they get those? According to the news, the Kapteynians used weapons that shot bullets. These were not bullets, almost causing me bodily harm. I came to the stairs at the other end of the hall and took them three at a time.

Not bad for a girl who skipped gym class.

I came to the bottom and looked down the hallway. The short guy was there but looking the wrong way. There was a fire extinguisher on the floor. I grabbed it and ran. The alien turned, but not in time. I swung the metal canister around. Nailing him right in the head. The little guy dropped like a rock. His weapon clanged to the floor. Laser beams began shooting past me. I was just yards away from the door and freedom.

Screw that and them.

I grabbed the alien weapon and spun. All the aliens were running up the hallway when the firing suddenly stopped. One raised his hand and yelled something. I pulled the trigger.

Four things happened. The weapon gave off a loud woofing sound. Then, a long, wide stream of swirling yellow and red beams shot through the barrel. This storm of colorful power engulfed the aliens and hallway. At least it looked like it as I flew back. The moment I pulled the trigger, I was literally lifted off my feet and thrown back down the hallway.

Talk about a kickback.

I landed on my butt. Yes, it hurt. I kept sliding back until I banged into the wall. I shook my head and looked at the weapon. I now knew why the other aliens didn't want this thing pointed in their direction. "Whoa. I like this gun."

I slowly climbed to my feet and rubbed my butt. A beeping made me look at the weapon still in my hand. A red light was now blinking. It would turn out to be a one-shot weapon. Then I looked up the hallway, or what was left of it.

If Principal Heller ever came back, she was going to be pissed. The other end of the hallway was scorched black. Tiny burning embers still floated around. There were little fires on the floor, wall, and ceiling. Light fixtures were dangling by wires. The lockers were now mostly melted blobs on the floor. There was also a hole in the back hall. I moved up and noticed there was nothing left of the aliens. There were small pools of silver scattered around, which I guessed to be all that remained of the aliens' weapons. I looked at the weapon again. "Geez, talk about overkill."

I turned back to the last alien lying behind me. He was spread-eagle across the floor. His helmet was lying a few feet away. There was a small pool of blood under his head.

Wow. I don't know my own strength.

The weapon gave off a few more beeps, and the light went out. I braced myself and pulled the trigger again.

Nothing.

My great luck just keeps going. Well, it wasn't all bad. I just kicked some alien butt and destroyed part of the school. All in all, it was not a bad day. I dropped the weapon and walked outside.

The home was just a couple of blocks away.

CHAPTER 12

Home. I walked up to the tiny house that was almost buried in snow. I climbed up a drift and kicked in a window to get inside. It was colder in here than outside. I took in the furniture that Dad had put together from Ikea. Poorly. I moved down the hallway to my room and peeked in. Snow covered most of my window, so it was pretty dark. Everything else looked in order. My bed. Unmade. My desk was cluttered with junk that had once seemed important to me. My posters of aliens and space seemed so wrong now. The big-foot posters were still cool. I had a big one on Mount Everest. I had planned to climb that sucker one day. I was still going to. Aliens or no aliens. That made me smile.

My cold toes reminded me why I was here. I went to my closet and pulled out my hunting jacket. It was waterproof, with fleece and a hood. The one big problem was that it was bright red. It was great to avoid being shot while hunting, but it was not a good thing in a white winter world filled with aliens and evil military types.

Next came jeans. Three pairs. I got all my thick socks and of course my boots. These babies were guaranteed to keep my tootsies warm and dry. I have three pairs of gloves. Thick mittens, thick-fingered and a fingerless pair. I had my own thermals, which I will save for later. I opened the trunk that sat at the back of my closet. I tossed aside the clothes and pulled out my knife. Mom and Dad didn't know about this. It was like a mini-version of Rambo's knife. Several packs of freeze-dried food that was so much better than the Army crap. I found two cans of spam and realized I was starving.

Yes, I like spam. I don't care what it is made of. I was thrilled when they came out with bacon spam and smoked spam. I will let you know they love the stuff in Hawaii. Can people who live in paradise be wrong? I don't think so.

The backpack was emptied. Then I undressed and redressed in jeans and one of my favorite flannel shirts that I rarely got to wear. I also put on socks, boots, and a knit cap. I was set to shove the fingered gloves into my jacket pockets and strap the knife onto my belt. Then I repacked, putting everything in, including one of the cans of spam. From out of the trunk came my compass, binoculars, and waterproof matches. I was ready.

I still needed a gun.

I went to the front room and started a small fire in the fireplace. After warming my hands, I went into the kitchen. I found the cast iron frying pan and some bread that wasn't stale. The big score was finding ketchup in the fridge—the one ingredient that makes anything tasty.

Soon, I was frying the spam in the fireplace and plotting my next move. I wondered what Reggan's Granddad's jeep was doing in front of the school. They were obviously making a run for it. Where would they be running to? The bunker? Texas? Mammoth was possible. That would be the smart move but in the wrong direction. I made my decision and then made a spam sandwich with ketchup.

Reggan's house was close by.

I feasted on spam sandwiches and warm coke that I found under my bed. After my meal, I stuffed the ketchup into my pack. It could help make the Army food edible.

I sat in front of the fire and thought how things had gotten so screwed up. My parents wanted me to sell my best friend for a plane ticket. I knew they were just scared, but there are things you just don't do, even if aliens invade.

I wondered how Reggan had changed. The best I could figure was she got the alien virus. Then, unlike everyone else, she had lived, but the virus had changed her. I just couldn't picture Reggan as some half-breed alien running around slaughtering people. She had the biggest heart in the world. I remember her dragging me down to the food bank to help. No. She wasn't a monster. But she did need my help. Right there, I made a vow to God. I do believe in God. I call myself an Agnostic-Deist. Still trying to figure out what that is. I am working out the details. Reggan's dad and I were constantly arguing about God.

Good times.

I considered it a small victory when he stopped being an atheist and became an agnostic. Reggan and her mom tried to take credit, but it was me. The atheists I knew were all jerks and angry about something. I think some people say they are atheists and just haven't thought it out. I heard one jerk say that agnostics were cowards afraid to become Atheists. I think it is the other way around. Life does get simpler if you say there is no God. Look around. Once again. Do you really think all this happened by sheer accident?

I don't think so.

It didn't happen in seven days, either. Sorry, getting off track here.

At some point, I fell asleep on the floor. It was the sound of trucks pulling up that woke me. I am a light sleeper, so I was instantly awake. I ran over to the window and stood on a table to see over the snow drift. There was an old Army truck parked in front of my house. Soldiers were jumping out and moving toward the house. A young sergeant was leading the charge. I spotted some people standing across the street. It never occurred to me that people still lived here.

Hiding in their houses. Waiting for this all to go away. It wasn't going to go away. Not anytime soon.

"All right! Listen up!" the sergeant yelled, his arms wrapped around his chest. He looked cold. He was not wearing thermals. We are looking for a teenager named Reggan Sobe. She's six feet..."

"Did you say six feet?" A soldier asked.

"Yes, six feet. Long red hair and freckles. She should be easy to spot." He continued. "The general wants her alive but will settle for dead. I want half of you to work the street. There is a reward. Cash money. Also wanted is a young blonde named Ellie. Sorry, didn't get the last name. Short and has an attitude. Apparently, it's quite clever. She escaped the camp through a roof panel and stole some army gear. There is a reward for her, too. But we need her alive. I suspect they think she can lead us to Sobe."

"Is this redhead the one they are calling Zero?"

"That is the one, gentlemen. So I suggest you take no chances with her. If I spot her, I am shooting her and asking questions later."

"Asshole," I muttered to myself and jumped down from the table. I grabbed my pack, ran back to the kitchen, and climbed onto the counter. I used the skillet to break out the window. For once, being small paid off. I shoved my pack through, then wiggled out into my backyard. I ran to the fence, pulling on my pack. The sounds of boots and muttering sounded close when I grabbed the fence and pulled myself over. I landed on my feet and looked around.

"Hey, I think someone just climbed that fence!"

"Footprints!"

I was off like a shot. I ran to the first open gate and ducked in, cursing that I was leaving a trail anyone could follow. I moved past the house and onto the street. Deep snow covered the road and lawns. I had no choice and plowed across the street. I just reached the other side when loud yells reached my ears. I looked back and saw three soldiers trudging after me. One aimed and fired.

Yikes!

I really needed a gun.

I heard one of the soldiers yell at the guy who took the shot. They actually stopped to argue. I ran around the house, hopped another fence through another snow-buried backyard, and stopped. I looked up and stared at the tree house. I ran out to the front of the house. The road had been cleared but was covered with slush.

No footprints.

But I am smarter than that. I carefully backed up, stepping in the footprints I left. I stopped when I could reach a low branch. I pulled myself up, which was no small feat with a backpack. Once I was on the branch, I crawled my way toward the treehouse. It was just a platform with plywood walls, but it would give me cover. The sounds of running feet and voices made me move faster. I heard another truck pull up. I reached the treehouse and literally fell into it just as a soldier came over the wall.

"Here! She went this way!"

I lay flat as the soldier climbed the wall and followed my tracks. I heard distant cursing when they reached the road. Another truck pulled up, and more yelling.

Finally, someone yelled for order.

"Okay, she is still in the neighborhood. It is not Zero. It could be her friend. Why else would she run? The streets are blocked. We have her trapped. Search every house, and I mean even the dog houses!"

I wish I had a gun.

CHAPTER 13

So here I am, lying in a tree house. The only good thing is I am warm. The bad news was the jacket I was wearing was bright red. There are soldiers with guns looking for me because they think I know where my best friend is. The joke here was I had no idea where Reggan was. To be honest, I have ideas, but I had no intention of sharing them with the morons running around below. As I lay, I knew I needed a plan. A good plan. You know, the kind of plan the heroine comes up with to save her butt and the day. That kind of plan. I thought for a moment, waiting for this plan to pop into my head.

Nothing.

I came up with some good ones where I was heroic and badass. They all involved a gun, but I don't have one of those.

I rolled onto my belly and peeked through a space between the plywood walls. The yard looked empty, but I could hear muffled yelling. I was smart enough to know that it was only a matter of time before they looked up and spotted the tree house. They were supposedly searching for dog houses.

"CLEAR!"

This made me look over the wall and down into the yard. Five soldiers came out of the house and moved toward the street. Four were dressed in regular Army green with standard-issue M16s. The one giving the orders was dressed in black fatigues and holding a sweet Colt M45. From up here, he looked a lot meaner than the other guys. Yeah, he was a killer. The kind of guy who would shoot a puppy and brag about it. Probably had tattoos all over his back and arms. As if tattoos make you cool.

The problem with tattoos is you are stuck with them for life. They don't age well. Trust me, I have seen my Granddad's tattoos. Most of them look like melted blobs of ink.

I waited for the puppy-killer to walk off, then climbed out of the tree house. I dropped to the ground, landing in the trail of boot prints, and moved toward the house. There were yelling voices all around me. I heard some trying to get over the back fence.

"Come on, man, move your fat ass!"

"I'm going! I'm going!"

"This is so sad, man; you are supposed to be a soldier."

I ran to the house and darted through the back door. I came into a small kitchen. All the cupboards and drawers had been pulled open. Broken bottles, open cans, and other trash were scattered over the floor. I went to the window over the sink and watched a chubby soldier struggle over the fence. He dropped down, crashing down into the snow, swore, and struggled up. The moron had lost his rifle in the deep snow and began to look for it. Two more soldiers came over and laughed. One looked up. "Hey, we better check that treehouse."

"Wait a sec. I've got to find my gun," Chubby said, laughing after pulling his M16 out of the snow. He began to brush it off. "Looks like they already checked the house."

"Yeah, yeah," one of the soldiers said, grabbing a low branch and pulling himself up. He managed to peek inside and dropped to the ground. "Empty. Let's check the house anyway. It has got to be warmer in there."

"Roger that," Chubby said.

I jumped back when the three men headed toward the door. I started to look for a place to hide, running to the front of the house. I peeked out the window. There were dozens of soldiers on the street looking for little old me. They were knocking on doors. If the person didn't answer fast enough, they kicked into the door.

Wow. The world was really going down the toilet.

The soldiers wore green or black. The guys in black seemed to be in charge, barking orders, insulting the guys in green, and even shoving them down into the snow.

You know. Typical bully stuff.

I spun when the back door opened and started for the bedroom. I came into the baby's room, and the pink walls and crib were my first clue.

Yeah, I am a regular Sherlock Holmes.

The good news was the crib had plenty of space for me and my pack. There was a blanket inside. I dropped the front railing down. Then, I used the blanket to give me more cover. It reminded me of the forts I built as a kid. I pushed my pack under the crib, then crawled under. It was cozy down here. I was tempted to take a nap, but that was not a good idea. I just laid there and listened. I could hear the soldiers banging around and talking. Occasionally laughing. I saw a pair of boots come into the room. I held my breath.

"What are you soldiers doing?"

"Searching the house, sir!"

"This house had been cleared. I have a man posted out front. I think I have some wimps who don't like the cold. I got a cure for that! Get your butts outside!"

What a jerk.

I listened to them walk out but stayed under the crib. It could be a trick. I didn't think these guys were that smart, but it was best not to take any chances. I lay there listening, my eyes slowly closing.

Suddenly, I woke up. I must have dozed off. I was lying in darkness and wondered how long I had been asleep. I must have been more tired than I thought. I groaned when I tried to move. My whole body had gotten stiff lying here, so it was still for too long. I pushed out my pack and crawled out. I shook my head and stretched, hoping the soldiers had moved on. I grabbed my bag and moved back to the front room. I could see the soldiers were still outside through the window, just not as many. Most were standing guard at different points on the street. I noticed a small group huddled in front of a house. Normal-looking families. Moms, dads, and kids. Three men in black were guarding them. They looked afraid and cold. A couple of the men looked pissed. The creeps could at least let them put on some jackets. A truck pulled up. The small group was forced to climb into the back. It was then I recognized a couple of the men. I didn't know their names, but I knew they were cops. Small town. I knew most of the cops.

It's a long story. Actually, there are a couple really good ones. There was this time I was out. No, I will tell you about it later.

It made me wonder if the other guys and maybe women were cops. It was hard to tell from here. I watched them all climb in. A young soldier climbed in behind them. I was waiting for the truck to pull away. A moment later, one of the cops jumped out, holding an M16. He shot the guys in black before they could react. He ran to the front, followed by another guy carrying a pistol. They took out some more soldiers. They pulled out the driver and jumped in. The guy with the gun fired off a few shots down the street just before the truck took off. I watched it take a corner, almost flipping over. It didn't, but the young soldier flew or maybe was tossed out the back and onto the road. All the other soldiers chased after the truck, firing at it.

"What the heck is going on?" I asked myself. Then, I realized this was a great time to make my escape. I snuck out the back and climbed the fence. I trudged down the street, acting like I belonged there. Distant gunfire told me that I was no longer a priority.

At least for now.

CHAPTER 14

I spent the rest of the night wandering around and hiding in several empty houses, avoiding several patrols. These guys seemed more interested in staying warm than really looking for me. I noticed the cold, too. We didn't get this kind of snow and cold in Cornwall.

In a movie, the aliens would cause this weather as part of their evil plot. It might just be a thought. That is how my mind works.

It was morning, and I was taking a short rest on a park bench across from the library. I was watching an army truck parked across the park. There was a small crowd of people surrounding the truck. A soldier was handing out bags of food. I noted six black soldiers had moved up behind the crowd. They were studying the crowd with their weapons down at their sides. Very relaxed. I wasn't fooled. These guys were puppy killers, too. They could bring up their weapons, spray the crowd, and not even feel bad about it. An officer was standing in an old army jeep and watching the crowd. He lifted a bullhorn to his lips.

"Ladies and gentlemen, we are only here to help and protect you. Right now, we need your help. We are looking for two young women. One goes by the name Reggan Sobe. She is also being called Zero. She's tall with long red hair and freckles. Sadly, she has been infected with an alien virus. This has mutated her into something very dangerous. She must be found. Preferably alive, but we will take her dead. There is a reward. The other one is named Ellie."

The officer looked down at the man driving the jeep. "We still don't have a last name on her?"

The driver shook his head.

"No last name. She's short with long blonde hair. Last seen wearing a red jacket. She has something of an attitude. Which could explain why she is helping Sobe. We need this girl alive. There is a reward."

I glanced at my bright red jacket and decided to leave. I stood up and walked down the street, stopping when I came to the library. I couldn't help myself. You may not believe this, but I am a big reader. Huge. I put away three or four books a week. I am talking about real books, not those Kindle things. Call me old-fashioned, but I like the feel of a book in my hands. Plus, you can flip the pages back and forth if you need to. I wandered into the small two-story building. It was so quiet. Not a good quiet. A lonely quiet. The kind of quiet that makes you sad and think. Thinking, in my opinion, is not always a good thing. Sometimes, you just have to be in the moment. You know. Take a breath and relish life.

I wandered up to the second floor and smiled. It looked like not one book had been touched. People are funny. They will rip a store or house apart for food but let their soul go hungry. I walked down the stacks, stopping and thinking. It made me sad that many kids my age had no idea who Agatha Christie was. Her stuff is dated, but she could write a good mystery. Christy stumped me more than once. Of course, she held back a clue or two. That wasn't really fair. Reggan and I used to argue about whether the Belgian guy was gay or not.

For the record, I am sure he was. The patent leather shoes were the big giveaway.

I stopped at another section. Dirk Pitt. Boy, we could use him and his buddy Al right now. Sean and Joe, too. Those guys were always saving the world. Sometimes, the plots were silly, but Clive could make you believe everything. He came up with some conspiracies that might just be true. The best part of his books was the villains always got theirs. Dirk not only saved the world but got the girl.

"Oh Dirk, where are you when we need you," I sighed, running my finger down the books. I looked around and realized this room was filled with heroes and heroines and the incredible adventures they had. The writers wrote about courage, honor, and the human spirit. The good stuff inside of us. I got angry. No dumb aliens or crazy general was going to stop me. As they have said in many movies, T.V. shows and books:

This is personal.

I snapped out of my thoughts when I heard the door open. Voices came up.

"I saw her come in here! Red jacket. Blonde hair!"

"You watch the back door! Dennis, stay here and watch where you point that thing!"

I peeked over the railing and groaned. Four guys had come into the library. Two were older men with fat bellies and beards. One was a kid about my age. The last one couldn't have been more than ten. He was holding a baseball bat. The older men were holding pump-action shotguns. The teenage boy was holding a double-barrel shotgun that looked too big for him. They were all dressed like hunters. Flannel shirts and jeans. I couldn't smell them but it looked like they hadn't bathed in a while.

Now what? These guys didn't look like the brightest bulbs in the package.

I looked at the rows and rows of shelves lined up so neat and high. I smiled and moved down the last aisle and climbed up using the shelves. I managed to get on top of the book shelf. I pulled off my pack and lay flat. The plan was to wait them out. I heard them come up still yelling.

"Okay! Okay. We got her trapped. You move down that aisle, and I will do this one. Move slow; I hear she is tricky."

I looked over at the other shelf and decided that I was tired of running, especially from these morons. I sat up and lowered myself down. I hopped onto the top of the shelf and put my boots against the shelf opposite me. I was surprised by how easily it tilted. The librarian was going to be so mad at me. I heard a loud creak. The bookcase I was pushing suddenly moved forward. It fell with a loud crash. I was left hanging onto the side of another bookshelf. I watched in awe as bookcase after bookcase slammed into each other like dominos. Crashing down with a loud roar. Dust flew up into a dusty cloud. I lost my grip and fell to the floor. A loud scream made me look up.

"OH CRAP! AWWWW!" A voice bellowed from under the destruction I had just created.

I looked over at the tilted pile of shelves and books, listening to the two men curse and call for help. The kid with the shotgun came charging up and ran right past me. He stopped and looked down. "Paw, you down there?"

"YES YOU DAMN FOOL! DON'T JUST STAND THERE. GET ME OUT OF HERE!"

I looked around and found an excellent thick atlas. I picked it up and walked right up to the kid. "Hey, kid, see the world!"

"What?" he said, turning with a stupid look on his face?

I slammed the book into his face. He dropped to the floor, grabbing his nose and screaming it was broken. I hit him again. No, not just for fun.

Well, maybe.

"You won't need this," I said, picking up his shotgun and looking at it. I was immediately disgusted. "Dude! Haven't you heard of gun maintenance? I probably just saved your life. This thing is filthy. It probably would have exploded if you had tried to shoot it. Rule one: Take care of your gun, and it will take care of you!"

"What's going on?" the guy under the shelves yelled.

"She broke my nose. She broke my nose." The kid was now sobbing and holding his nose.

"I think my arm is broken!" the other man yelled from somewhere. "Call 911!"

"There is no 911 anymore!" I yelled, still looking at the weapon with disgust. I was about to climb onto the shelves and see if I could get one of the pump shotguns when a scream made me look around. The young kid was charging me with the baseball bat raised over his head. He seemed so determined. I shook my head in disbelief. "Are you kidding me?"

I waited until he was almost before me and about to swing. I stepped out of the way and stuck out my foot. He tripped over my foot and landed on top of his brother. Both screamed and yelled. The young one rolled off, glared at, and tried to grab the bat. I stomped on his hand and pushed the shotgun barrel in front of his face. "Seriously?"

"Boy, if you didn't have a gun!" he growled.

"If I didn't have a gun, I would have to kick your butt all over this room." I smiled.

"Would not!"

"Would too!" God, I was back in kindergarten. I was tempted to smack the kid, but I had a thing about hurting idiots. They were just so stupid and sad. I looked around, grabbed the kid by the back of his jacket, and literally dragged him over to the bathroom. I shoved him in and used a table to block the door. He began to bang on it.

"Hey, don't leave me in here! It stinks! It really stinks!"

"Good!" I snapped and returned to the teenager still holding his nose. Now, he was crying. He had an ammo belt draped across his chest. I pulled this off. He protested until I threatened to hit him again.

"Wimp!" I said, and climbed on top of the pile of shelves and books, looking for the pump action shotguns. The men below screamed when I stepped on them.

Poor babies.

I spotted the butt of one of the shotguns, but it was stuck under a shelf. I was figuring out how to get it out when more voices came up from below. "Oh man, I can't catch a break."

I jumped over the shelves, making the men yell and curse again. Junior was still holding his nose and was crying. God, what a wimp. I looked over the railing and groaned. Two soldiers dressed in black walked in and stopped. They were both holding MP5s. I could really use one of those.

"I just want to see why those jerks ran in here."

"They were running pretty fast. You hear that? That someone crying?"

I glared at the kid and ran. I stopped long enough to grab my pack. There was a back staircase that led to the library's back door. I crept down these and watched the two soldiers trot up to the second floor. I slipped out the back door and tried to nonchalantly walk up the street holding a too-big double barrel shotgun.

No one gave me a second look.

CHAPTER 15

An hour later, I was in the back of the BIG 5 sporting goods store. I lucked out and found a gun cleaning kit and a nice new jacket that was a dull green. It's much better than bright red. The shotgun was taking forever to clean. Turns out most of the shells in the belt were rotted and useless. I had only ten shots. Before cleaning it, I found a hacksaw in a hardware store and sawed it off the barrel. Then, after some thought, I shortened the stock. It was now much more practical.

After a quick search, I found a camp stove and fry pan. In the employee lounge, I found some English muffins. I fried some spam and put it on the muffins. I added ketchup, and I had a feast. I washed it with warm coke, looking longingly at the coffee machine.

Man, I could use some coffee.

This made me laugh. Reggan must be going insane. She is the biggest coffee addict I know. Not the sweet, wimpy stuff. She loves good, strong coffee with milk and a lot of sugar. My bestie couldn't get through the day without at least five huge cups. The funny thing was her mom didn't want her to drink coffee, so Reggan had to do it behind her back. I have known Reggan to crawl out of her bedroom window at night to get her fix.

"Aw, Reggan, I love you and miss you. I am so going to find you."

I figured I had been here too long and decided to move on. The next stop was Reggan's house. I didn't think she would be there, but I had to check. After stuffing my hair under a knit cap, I shouldered the pack and headed out. The streets were empty, except for the occasional person rushing somewhere. They all crossed the street when they saw me. I was holding a shotgun. I kept looking over my shoulder, sure that the Army would show up and grab me. Even I had to admit I had been pretty lucky. The snow was pretty deep, but it had stopped falling, and the streets had been plowed. It made the journey easier.

Reggan had the nicest house. It was so small-town. I think they called it a Victorian. Painted white with blue trim. One story had a porch that even had a porch swing. I had spent many hours sitting and even sleeping in it. The old memories swept over me and made me feel sad. I was brought back from my trip down memory lane by loud laughing and swearing. I double-checked my shotgun and climbed to the steps. Then, I peeked inside the front window. Four guys that might have been college-age were slumped on the sofa. They were passing a bottle filled with foamy gold liquid. The world is coming to an end, and these jerks are getting drunk.

Why was I not surprised?

One of the guys struggled to his feet, laughing. Saying he had to take a wiz. I watched as he staggered over to a corner and unzipped. He was peeing in my friend's house. My anger took over. I kicked in the door and rushed in. "Get the hell out of here!

"Hey, hey, there's no need for that. We're all friends," one of the guys on the sofa laughed, raising his hands in mock surrender. The guy in the corner didn't even turn around. This really burned me. I rushed over and slammed his head against the wall. He cried in pain, dropping to his knees. I looked around and spotted a rag on the floor. I snatched it up and tossed it onto his lap.

"CLEAN UP!" I snarled, poking him in the chest to make my point. When he didn't move fast enough, I slapped him. Out of the corner of my eye, I noticed movement. The three other guys were on their feet and moving toward me. Granted, they all looked like they were about to fall down again. I pointed the shotgun and growled. "GET OUT!"

"Wait," one said.

I fired one shell into the floor by their feet and gave them my best Arnold glare. You may find this hard to believe, but I have perfected this look. Back when I was a typical high school kid, no one messed with me.

Okay, maybe I wasn't normal, but still, no one messed with me.

The three guys jumped back, seeming to get the message, and ran for the door. It was so sad. They kept falling over each other, trying to get out. Finally, they got out. I went to the window, watched them slip, and slid down the street. I turned back to the last moron. He was still sitting on his butt, looking at the rag. I stormed over, grabbed the back of his jacket, and forced him to kneel. "CLEAN THAT UP!"

Once again, he didn't move fast enough for me, so I kicked him. He grunted but finally got the message and started to wipe the floor. The moron started crying and saying I was being crazy. "No one lives here! We ain't hurting anyone! The girl turned into some kind of freak. We were hoping she'd come back. There is a reward for her."

"God, how stupid are you?" I yelled and grabbed the back of his jacket, and made him crawl over to the door, giving his butt a few more kicks. We got outside, and I shoved him down the stairs. Then aimed the shotgun. "You come back here, and I will kill you. You tell your stupid friends the same thing!"

He started to cry and limp off down the street. I was so tempted to put him out of his misery because, in this new world, he was surely going to die. But there was my whole not-hurting-idiots thing. Watching him go, I wondered if I would have to change that policy. "MORON!"

I went back into the house and into the kitchen. I found some cleaner under the sink and a sponge. Then, I returned to the corner and cleaned it up. As I rubbed the floor, tears came to my eyes. I sobbed like a baby in a few seconds as I kept cleaning. I have no idea how long I scrubbed, but it ended with me banging the walls with both fists. Then I crumbled into a ball. It took a few minutes to get control of myself. I forced myself up, took deep breaths, and wiped away the tears. "You are tougher than this! You are tougher than this! You are strong! Get it together! Reggan needs you!"

It was only then I noticed the bullet holes. Not just a few bullet holes, but dozens. The walls and floor were peppered with holes. A lot of the furniture had been splintered and, in some cases, destroyed by gunfire. I went back into the kitchen. More bullet holes and destroyed cabinets. An unfinished cup of hot chocolate and a cookie were on the table. Someone had left in a hurry. I rushed back to Reggan's room and started to search her closet. Her hunting jacket and jeans were gone. The screen had been knocked out of the window. Had Reggan gotten out? She must have. The Army wouldn't be looking for her if she hadn't escaped. "Okay, think. Think. There was a firefight here. They got out! The jeep by the high school. Reggan and at least her granddad had gotten as far as the school. Then what? Go to Texas. Yes, but not without supplies. Mammoth! They headed for Mammoth! Yes!"

Mammoth was a small town about twenty-eight miles from here. What was in Mammoth, you ask? You have to understand that Reggan's granddad was in the Vietnam War and came back a lot smarter. Some people thought he was crazy. But in my book, he came back brilliant. Real smart. He became what was known as a prepper. One of those supposed crazy guys who got ready for the end of the world.

Yeah, who is crazy now? I bet you wish you had a bunker filled with food, water, and weapons.

The guy not only built an honest-to-God bunker but got together with a bunch of other guys. They pooled their money and built a super bunker under a sporting goods store in Mammoth. It was loaded with weapons, food, and clothing. It even had solar power for lights and stuff. I told you these guys were brilliant. The deal was if the end of the world came or aliens invaded and you were a member, you could go to the bunker and get what you needed. You may ask how I know about this. I am a member. I donated three hundred bucks.

I am no dummy.

Now I have someplace to go. A place where I can get a much better gun.

Off in the distance, I heard the sounds of trucks. As far as I knew, only the Army had trucks. It was time to go.

CHAPTER 16

I watched from behind a tree as the men in black charged into Reggan's house. The four morons were standing across the street.

That's another reason I should have killed them.

Live and learn.

No, I really wouldn't have killed them. Well, maybe I'd have shot them. Okay, maybe kick their drunken butts.

I crept away, leaving the Army to do its thing. I moved over to another street. Always listening. I glanced up, noting the sun was going down. It would be stupid to start hiking to Mammoth in the middle of the night. I needed a place to bunk down for the night. There were plenty of houses, but not all of them were empty. Then, the Army could bring in more troops to do another house-by-house. I have been really lucky so far. I needed a place where they wouldn't look for me. I came to the top of a snow drift and saw my answer.

Frankie the Fighting Otter.

The Oregon Tech Football stadium. It was huge. There had to be tons of places to hide. Maybe even some food somewhere. I glanced back at the muffled yelling and took off. It was only a few blocks away. The upside to living in a small town is that almost everything is within walking distance. I entered the parking lot, surprised at how many cars there were. Most had been there quite a while since they were now buried in snow. There were paths through the snow around the cars like people had been going in and out. This made it easier but made me nervous. I kept glancing around, staying on my toes. It was when I was passing a car and looked inside. I gasped and jumped back, bringing up the shotgun. It took me a few seconds to realize the face in the window belonged to a dead woman. I stepped closer and peeked inside. She wasn't alone. Two small kids sat in the front seat. This may surprise you. These were the first dead bodies that I had seen. I stood there too long, trying to figure out why they were dead. I couldn't see any wounds or any sign of the alien virus. Did they just sit in there and let the winter take them? I put my hand on the window. "I am sorry. You deserved better than this."

We all did.

I moved into the stadium, looking forward. The thought of other families in the cars was too much for me. I walked past the gates and out into the field.

I should have never come here.

I stood looking down. The football field was buried in snow, but I could still see the tops of tents. Tents that had been put up to help the sick. Now, I suspected they were filled with dead bodies. Bodies were lying on top of the snow. More were half buried. They were all frozen, which made them look even creepier. I turned away and stumbled back. More dead bodies. They were lying on the seats, in the aisles, and on the steps. My eyes came to the massive painting of the Fighting Otter. The big stupid smile on his face. I ran into the hallway, stopped, and threw up. I kept throwing up even after my stomach was empty. Tears ran down my face, and I sobbed.

So this was war.

The part of war you didn't think about or want to see. These weren't soldiers. They were just people. People who probably never hurt anyone. The military called it collateral damage. I called it wrong.

So wrong.

I blamed the aliens. Why had they come so far just to do this? Couldn't they have just asked for help? Did they just come down and decide that we Earthlings weren't needed? Then, I blamed the Army. It looked like they were doing some collateral damage of their own.

As you have probably figured out, I am a big conspiracy buff. I'm like Agent Mulder. The truth is out there, but Big Brother doesn't want you to know it. I want to go on record right now. I am pretty sure that our government is using this alien invasion to its advantage. For all I know, they could be working with the aliens. You just remember that when I say I told you so!

I left the stadium as fast as I could, careful not to look into any more cars. Soon, I was just running—down street after street. I finally stopped, exhausted. I was panting and gasping like an old woman.

Okay, I should have taken those gym classes.

I finally caught my breath. I was dizzy and needed to sit down, but not on the street. A steep staircase led up to a house sitting on top of a small hill. I pulled out my water bottle and drained it. Then I climbed the steps. Yes, huffing and puffing. The house was a small but expensive looking place. The carport was empty, but I moved around the house and peeked through the windows. The place seemed empty. The door was unlocked. I took this as an invitation to come on it and take what I wanted. What I wanted was to sit down and catch my breath.

No luck there.

I needed to make sure the place was empty. The living room looked messy, but I wondered if this was normal or if the people had left in a hurry? The kitchen table still had dirty dishes on it. Four people had eaten eggs and bacon without cleaning up. The cupboards were empty of anything I could use. There was food in the fridge and freezer, but it was questionable. In a top cupboard over the fridge, I really scored. Two gallons of water, a One Crunch bar, four Snickers, and my favorite, six Kit Kat bars. I stuffed all the candy but one Kit Kat into my pack and ate the other while refilling my water bottle. I found some more empty bottles in their recycling bin. I filled them and put them all into my pack.

There were three bedrooms in the back. One had bunk beds and looked like a boy's room. It looked messy, but the drawers were pulled open. Things looked like they had been tossed onto the floor. Typical boy's room. I moved on to the parents. It was in the same mess. Not typical. My guess was this family was long gone. The office was in the very back. I stepped in and smiled. A portable CD player with headphones sat right on top of the big desk. I scooped it up and hit play.

Nothing.

Dead batteries. I began to look through the desk drawer. Whoever owned this desk was very organized. There had to be batteries. Guys like this stockpiled batteries. I opened the bottom drawer and smiled. It was filled with double-A batteries still in their plastic packages, plus extra pairs of headphones. I tore open one of the packages and loaded the CD player. Some classical music came out. Not my was no ttaste.

Don't judge.

I pulled out the Taylor Swift CD I found and replaced the CD in the player. I closed my eyes and hit play. Taylor's voice filled my ears. She was singing about New York. I slumped into a chair that was surprisingly comfy and smiled. Reggan and Trisha were always talking about going to New York. Los Angeles. Actually, any big city. They couldn't wait to get out of Cornwall. I was on the fence about that. Sure, I wanted to leave Cornwall and see the world. New York sounded too intense for me. From what I had seen on TV, they were kind of rude and genuinely loved swearing. I don't swear that much. I would watch kids at school throw out F bombs and try to sound like those rappers. Trust me, you haven't seen anything funnier than some small-town white kid trying to imitate a rapper. The sad thing is they actually thought they were cool. I found that most people stop listening when you use curse words to make your argument. One time I was walking down the hallway, and some girl I didn't even know called me a bitch. I kept walking, and then she called me a bitch again, using the F word with it. Some people just don't know when to stop. I turned back and walked right up to her and nicely said. "What did you say?"

She repeated it, but this time with a lot more swearing and downright insulting words. Then she smiled.

I punched her.

Laid her out on the floor and looked down. She looked totally shocked. I moved closer and said. "Say it again."

By this time, a crowd had formed. Yes, phones were out. Luckily, no one caught the punch—just the results. I waited. She rubbed her nose and jaw. Then she glared at me and said, "You're crazy!"

"I can live with that. Just remember that next time you insult me," I said and walked away. By the time a teacher showed up, I was long gone. Next period, I was called to the principal's office and denied everything. My—my against hers. All those kids in the hallway, including her two friends, said they hadn't seen anything.

That's high school. No one wants to be a rat.

Taylor finished. I clicked forward to another song about getting out of the woods. It seemed right. The music video was really cool. I do love wolves. I just sat there and enjoyed. Miss Swift was taking me away to a better and happier place.

CHAPTER 17

I woke up in the chair. It took a second to realize where I was. I rubbed my eyes and looked out the window. It was almost dark. Another day lost. Since no one had found me, I decided to stay here for the night.

Luckily, the house had a fireplace. I made a fire and used pans from the kitchen to boil water for dinner. The freeze-dried beef stew wasn't that bad, especially after adding ketchup. I did find some tea and had some of that. Not a big fan, but at this point, caffeine is caffeine. I listened to some more Taylor while I ate. There had to be someplace I could score some more CDs. I do enjoy Miss Swift, but variety is the spice of life. I checked out the bookcase. There was a Dirk Pitt I had yet to read and a couple of Stephanie Plum novels I had meant to get into. A New Jersey ex-lingerie saleswoman turned bounty hunter. Sounds like fun to me.

I took the books into the guest bedroom and read until the sun went down. I was tempted to use my flashlight, but I only had two batteries left. Darkness engulfed me, and I felt sad. I missed Reggan and Trisha. With the shotgun at my side and fully dressed, I lay back and slept.

It was the loud bang that made me sit up. I grabbed the shotgun and looked around. The sun was up. I heard another bump and waited. It was time to leave. I rolled off the bed, glad I slept in my clothes. There was moving, followed by cursing. I pulled on my backpack and crept to the door. The noises were coming from the kitchen. It was probably someone just looking for food. I was hoping they would leave.

What to do?

I could wait or go. I looked around out the door and down the hallway. More crashing. Someone wasn't happy. My eyes drifted toward the front door. Then a dark figure came into the hallway. I jumped back and backed into a corner, hoping the shadows would hide me. My thumb pulled back the hammers of the double barrel shotgun. One finger rested on the trigger. I didn't want to fire both barrels. I watched as an older man walked right past the door. He went into the office. I decided to take my chance. Another glance down the hallway. Then, backing up to the door. I kept looking back at the same time. I stopped when a raspy voice made my head whip around.

"Now, what the hell do we have here?"

The old man stood at the end of the hallway. He wore tattered jeans, two sweaters, a shirt, and a long duster that had seen better days. A red checkered hunting hat with flaps was pulled down over his curly hair. A messy beard covered his chin, making him look less human. I glanced down at the wet sneakers. My guess? This guy was cold, hungry, and scared. I brought the shotgun up and aimed it. The barrels shook. I backed up until I was almost to the door. There was a small foyer. Then, the door. I would have run if the door was open. It wasn't. "Don't move! I am just trying to leave. The house is yours."

"Leave?" He said with smile. "Why you leaving? It looks to me like you could use some help. I could be that help."

"No thanks, I'm doing fine," I said, my voice cracking. I heard a click and glanced at the door. Did he have friends? "Just stay right there and let me go. This doesn't have to end up with you getting shot."

"Aw, sweetie, you ain't going to shoot me," he said, stepping forward and reaching inside his jacket.

"Don't!" I yelled, taking a tighter grip on the shotgun. The hairs on the back of my neck stood up. My mouth was suddenly dry. Tears ran down my cheeks. "I will shoot you!"

"Come on, honey, I bet you have never shot a gun. That thing has a hell of a kickback."

"I have lost count of the times I have fired a gun, and that does include a shotgun," I said, my voice sounding hitchpitched and cracking even more. A sob came out. What was with this guy calling me honey and sweetie? "Show me your hand! Now!"

Did the door move?

Out of the corner of my eye, I saw movement. I jumped back as the door flew open. Suddenly, someone was running in with a pistol. He was yelling for me to drop my gun. I whirled around and watched him aim the pistol. I screamed and pulled the trigger. The blast of the shotgun filled the room. Things on the wall shook. Dust came down from the ceiling. The guy with the pistol flew back out the door.

A loud scream filled my ears.

"YOU KILLED MY BOY!"

I spun around. The old man was charging up the hall with what looked like a meat cleaver. His eyes were huge, filled with rage. I could see the spit coming out of his mouth. I pulled the other trigger. The blast stopped him cold. More dust fell down from the ceiling. He just stood there, looking surprised. Without realizing it, I had ejected the two shells and was reloading. The old man finally dropped to the floor. I backed out of the door, stepping over the body. It was then I spotted the pistol lying by the man's hand.

No, not a man.

More a boy. He couldn't have been more than eighteen, maybe twenty. His clothes were just like the old man's. A mismatch of things put together to keep warm. I reached down, trying to accept the fact I had just killed two men. I told myself I had no choice. I kept telling myself this as I reached down and picked up the pistol.

It was too light.

I looked at it. It wasn't a real pistol. It was a plastic toy. The dead guy had been threatening me with a toy. I looked down at him and screamed. "Why would you do that? Why would you be so stupid! STUPID!"

I turned and staggered away, dropping to my knees. Once again, I threw up. Tears flooded my eyes, and my head hurt. I finally wiped away the tears and got up, looking back at the young man. "STUPID! STUPID!"

I got control of myself, realizing someone may have heard the shotgun. I forced myself to walk away but still kept saying stupid over and over. I reached the street and walked, pulling out a bottle of water. Suddenly, I was so thirsty. I emptied two bottles while walking. After a while, I stopped and looked around. I was standing in front of Fred Meyers. How had I ended up here?

Since I was here, I may do some shopping. The glass doors were all broken. I didn't expect to find much, but it wouldn't hurt to look. As expected, the place was pretty ransacked. Almost all the shelves were empty. I scored two cans of peaches and a box of pancake mix. This gave me an idea. I went back to the kitchenware isle and found a flat grill pan. The camping gear was on the second floor. It had almost been picked clean. Surprisingly, there was a camp stove. I set it and made myself some pancakes. It would have been better with butter and syrup, but beggars can't be choosers. I sat at a counter that looked out over the rest of the store to watch the front doors. My eyes couldn't help but drift over the empty aisles. Trash on the floor. It reminded me of those ghost towns I had seen on TV. Empty. All the people are gone and not coming back.

I killed two men this morning. It didn't matter if I was right or wrong. I had killed them. Alien war or not. I had killed them. The old Ellie was dead. I was the new Ellie who was going to not only survive but find my friend.

I finished my pancakes.

CHAPTER 18

I was packing and heading for the door when I stopped. A big sign announced that CDs were on sale. Free sounded good to me. I was surprised to find the CD racks almost untouched.

For the record. No beer or cigarettes. Not that I smoked or drank. I just found that interesting. All the flat-screen TVs and PlayStations were gone, too.

People can be so stupid when they are afraid.

Like those guys this morning.

Yes, I went to S and found all of Taylor's CDs. This should not surprise you. I also grabbed some Led Zeppelin, AC/DC, some Beatles and of course some Rolling Stones. No rap. I am not sure if I wasn't into rap because everyone else was or if I just didn't like it. I put the CDS into my pack and decided I had been here too long. It was time to hit the road,

Mammoth was my next stop.

I didn't put on the headphones until I was well out of town. I was tempted to just follow Highway 99—the Army had even cleared it—but going cross-country was my best bet. I was a wanted woman, but I wasn't worried. With my compass in hand and my incredible sense of direction, there was no way I was getting lost.

I made my way out of town, looking for one of the trails I had used back in the old days. Old days? God, how long had it been? A month? Two? Seemed like years.

It was a pain wading through the snow, but I took this as a good sign. There were no tracks, no holes. I felt safer once I made it into the trees. The snow was not as deep, so my pace increased. At this point, I decided it was time for some music.

Led Zeppelin, if you're keeping track.

I was making good time, but the sun was setting. The clouds overhead made the night come sooner. I looked around and realized

I knew this area. There should be a small cabin not far from here. I checked my compass. Really, I didn't have to, but you can't ever be too safe, especially with aliens and crazy army guys running around.

I was tramping along when I heard the voices. I froze and listened. More than one.

Kids? At least one.

I cocked my hammers and moved very slowly forward. The voices were coming from a clearing just up ahead. I crept up to a big tree and peeked around.

There was an older man with two small kids. He was about forty, maybe older, with chocolate-colored and graying hair. Thick glasses rested on his nose, making him look like one of my math teachers. He was wearing cotton pants, a shirt, and a windbreaker. Yes, he looked very cold, but not as cold as the two kids kneeling by a tree. They weren't dressed any better than him. They all had their arms wrapped around themselves.

"I'm sorry, kids," the man said, looking very sad. It looks like another night in the woods. I'll try to get a fire going."

"I'm really cold and hungry, Daddy," the small girl said, her voice trembling. She was looking around at the tall trees like they were going to attack her. "I want to go home."

"We can't go home!" the older boy said with bitterness.

"Jason!" the man said. Then he sighed. It was the sigh of a man who was way out of his depth. He wanted to help his kids but needed help figuring out what to do. "Honey, we are all cold and hungry."

"What the heck you doing up here?" I asked, stepping out but bringing up my shotgun. "You're not going to survive the night out here."

They all jumped up. Both kids moved behind their dad. The girl wrapped her arms around his leg, looking at me with huge eyes. Huge brown eyes filled with fear and hope. The kind of look that only six or younger can give you that breaks your heart. The boy glared at me. He couldn't have been more than ten. Trying hard to be brave for his sister. The man looked nervous. I knew he was taking in the small blonde girl holding the shotgun. "Who are you? We don't want any trouble."

"Looks like you have enough trouble," I said, looking around. "You alone? Why are you here? I know Cornwall isn't safe, but it is much more dangerous up here. There are bears, and they are hungry."

"Bears don't attack people unless provoked," the man said with a little more authority. "Who are you?"

"If they are hungry enough, they will attack," I said, not mentioning my name. I was a wanted woman. "I am the one with the gun, so you should answer first."

"We had no choice," he said, still looking nervous. "Two days ago, the Army showed up at my house. Fortunately, we were across the street looking for food. I have no idea what they wanted. I watched them beat my next door neighbor. An old man who never hurt anyone. He kept saying he had no idea where we were. "

"A lot of that going around," I said, thinking of the puppy killers dressed in black. I was tempted to move on but I couldn't just leave them. "You better come with me."

"I think we'll be fine by ourselves," he said.

"There is a cabin about two hundred yards that way," I said, pointing with the shotgun. "That's where I am heading. You can come along or stay here and freeze your butts off."

I trudged off toward the cabin I hoped was still there. All three stayed by the tree, watching me. After a few minutes, I came into the clearing. Ron Davis' cabin was still standing. Ron was an old hunting buddy. It looked deserted. Knowing Ron, he went south to Texas. He had family down there. I crept up the small cabin. It looked like something a pioneer had built with logs, a wood shingle roof with a stone chimney at one end. I pushed the door. It swung open. It was a two-room deal. The main room served as a living room and kitchen. The furnishing was stuff that Ron made or picked at Goodwill. The kitchen has cupboards, a counter, a sink, and a hand pump. There was no electricity, and the bathroom was an outhouse Ron had built along with the cabin.

I moved to the one door and pushed it open. An old brass bed took up most of the room. Satisfied I was alone, I took off my pack and looked around. A quick check of the cupboards rewarded me with two cans of baked beans and a can of cooked beef. I worked the handle of the pump. It groaned like an old man, but water finally came out of the spout. I moved to the stone fireplace, laying my shotgun down beside me. It was a massive thing made of heavy stone with a nicely carved mantle. I started to reach for some kindling when I heard someone behind me. I laid my hand on the shotgun. "I went through a lot of trouble to get this. People got hurt, and for the record, I am much tougher than I look."

I turned and looked right into the face of the ten-year-old, whose small hand was reaching for my shotgun. The kid jumped back. I smiled at him. You got guts, kid. I will give you that. Now back off."

"You know how to make a fire?" Jason asked, moving closer.

"Don't you?" I asked, taking some of the kindling from the stack by the fireplace. "You better learn. I don't think the power will come back anytime soon. First, stack the kindling on the grate here. Small pieces first. You see, I am kind of making a teepee here. That is so the air can flow through it. Fire needs air to burn. Now we stack three logs like this."

"So the air can get through," he said with a smile. "I saw those guys on TV make fire with some sticks. Can you do that?"

"Yes, I can," I said, pointing to the box of long matches sitting on the mantle. "Fortunately, we have fire sticks. Now, this is important. Some people just ball up the newspaper and shove it under the grate. You don't get a good burn that way."

I took some newspaper stacked by the kindling and began to rip it into strips. "I make thin strips and then fluff them up like this."

"Okay," Jason said, watching me push the pile of newspaper strips under the grail. He took down the box and pulled a match out. "Can I light it?"

"Be my guest. You know, this is one of the things that separates us from the animals. We can make fire," I said, watching him light the newspaper. It flared up and began to burn. It only took a couple minutes for the wood to catch. "Not much else separates us. In some ways, animals are a lot smarter than we are. Good job. We won't be cold tonight."

"JASON!"

I grabbed my shotgun and brought it up. The father was standing there with a log in his hands. He looked terrified until he spotted his son. Then he relaxed and looked at the fire.

I got up, went into the kitchen, and found a large pot with a handle that looped across the top. The father was still standing by the door. The daughter pushed in, saw the fire, and her brother trotted over and began to warm her hands.

"You make this?" she asked, looking at her brother.

"I helped," he said with a smile.

"Your son came to steal my shotgun. I think we have come to agreement that it is mine and fire is a good thing," I said, opening the cans of beans. Progress. You no longer needed a can opener. Just pull the tag. I dumped both cans into the pot. Then, I added the beef stew.

Never said I was a gourmet cook.

I stirred the mixture. Then, I carried it over to the fireplace. The pot in one hand. The shotgun in the other. I wasn't born yesterday, and this kid got his guts from someone. Probably his mother. "You staying or going? Whatever you're going to do, do it now and close the door. The heat is getting out."

"My name is Bennett. That's Julia, and you have met Jason," Bennett said, closing the door and moving toward the fire.

"There are some quilts in the bedroom closet. There might be some warmer clothes. Ron was a big guy, so they won't fit, but you will be warm," I said, putting the pot on the metal arm mounted into the stone. I swung in until it hung just over the flames. "You guys can have the bed. I will take the sofa. Oh, just so everyone knows. I am a very light sleeper."

"Understood. There will be no problem. You have demonstrated that you are more than capable of taking care of yourself," Bennett said, getting up and moving toward the bedroom. "I didn't get your name?"

"It's Ellie."

"Ellie," he said, turning. "Reggan Sobe's friend?"

CHAPTER 19

"You know Reggan?" I asked, looking over at the man with genuine surprise and suspicion.

"I was one of her doctors," Bennett said. "I was there when she came out of the coma. Everyone was shocked. My supervisor, Dr. Willis, was the first to realize how important this was. We created the cure together."

"For that, I thank you," I said, standing up. "I've heard rumors that my friend..."

"She has not mutated into a monster," Bennett snapped. He must have remembered who he was talking to. "She talked about you a lot. Reggan hoped that you had lived. She said if you lived, nothing would stop you from finding her."

"You said she changed. How?"

"She ran off before we could complete all our tests," he said. "We suspected her senses were heightened. Almost cat-like. I'm making that comparison because of her eyes."

"What's wrong with her eyes?" I said, moving closer. "She blind or something?"

"On the contrary. We suspected that Reggan's eye sight drastically improved. Willis suspected that she had some kind of night vision. She left the hospital a little annoyed with us."

"I guess she got tired of being poked and probed. You know, lab rat stuff."

"Then it all happened so fast," Bennett said, ignoring my poke at his occupation. "The Army just showed up looking for her. That same night, the aliens attacked her house. Her parents used the confusion to run off."

"Wait. The aliens attacked her house?" I asked. "Just her house? Why?"

"You don't know?"

"Know what?"

"The aliens are dying. The very virus they brought with them mutated. That's what viruses do. They mutate and adapt. Always looking for another way to spread. The incubation period is much longer, and the symptoms appear much slower. An alien could have it for weeks, even months, before he gets sick."

"I get it; the aliens want Reggan for a cure." Suddenly, I saw why the Army wanted her so badly. "And the army doesn't want the aliens to get it."

"I don't know what the army really wants," Bennett said, going to the fireplace and stirring the food. "General Watershaw is in charge now. I have serious doubts about the man's sanity."

"I have met the man. Trust me, he is crazy," I said, taking it all in. Reggan was alive and had super senses, which could be a good thing. Those are probably keeping her alive. Then I remembered her grandad's jeep by the school. You said she disappeared after the alien attack."

"Yes, that very night. I don't know all the details, but she fled with her parents and grandfather. I do know they made it into the mountains. There was a huge battle between the aliens and the Army. She used that as a cover to escape. Sadly, her father and grandfather weren't so lucky."

"Mr. Sobe is dead? Her grandad is dead?" I gasped, just standing there for a moment. "Are you sure?"

"Yes, the bodies were brought in for autopsy. We were still trying to figure out how your friend survived. We found out too late. Whoever was running things didn't appreciate us finding the cure. They shut down the labs."

"When I was at a camp. A soldier told me he suspected his commanding officer was keeping the cure under lock and key."

"It was the same in Cornwall, but gallons of the cure had already been shipped out. Then, the rank and file noticed the high-ranking officers weren't getting sick. Loud disagreements. Shots were fired. Officers died. Then suddenly Watershaw announced they had the cure."

"I knew it. I knew it!" I growled. "The government is working with the aliens. It goes back to Roswell. I wouldn't be surprised to find our government has been buddies with the aliens for decades."

"That is a pretty big leap," Bennett said, checking the beans and beef. "I agree something is going on. Jason, see if you can find some dishes and utensils."

"You know what I think," I said, going to the cupboard and opening it. I handed down plates to Jason and then pointed to a drawer. He opened it and started to take out spoons and forks. "I think the Army was at your house to tie up some loose ends. You are one of the guys who made the cure. Maybe the aliens will try to grab you. Safer to have you dead."

"No, no. I just helped make it. Willis was the genius behind it. He was the one who got local companies to manufacture it and then ship it out."

"Where is Dr. Willis now?" I asked, still trying to put it all together.

"I was just wondering that myself. Thank you, son," he said, taking the plates and putting food on them. He handed a plate to each kid and then looked at me. "I didn't want to believe it but you saying it out loud. It makes it all too real. Willis is one of those men who care more about the science than the people. Do we have anything to drink?"

"Let's see," I said, taking another look around. My first search was just a quick look around. I found a bottle of root beer and a bag of coffee. I looked through the pots and pans. I came up with an old fashioned coffee pot. "Yes, we have coffee and warm root beer."

"God, I could use a cup of coffee," Bennett said, coming over. He looked around for glasses. Found two and filled then with root beer. He took back the kids. Both asked for more food. "You better get some before the two bottomless pits eat it all."

"Let's get the coffee going," I said, putting water in the pot and filling the metal filter cup with coffee. I was spooning the black powder in when I had a thought. "You said just Reggan's dad and grandad were killed? What about her mother?"

"I don't know. I would assume the family were all together," Bennett said.

Reggan's mom was a kindergarten teacher. She never went camping with us. She hated the outdoors. So Reggan was not only on the run but protecting her mother. Reggan needs me more than I realized.

I looked at Bennett, first at him and then at his kids, who were happily eating the food and even laughing. What was I going to do with them? I couldn't just leave them here. I walked over to the fireplace and hung the coffee pot on another hook. My stomach grumbled. I made myself a plate of food and sat down on the sofa. I ate the food, which tasted better than it looked.

Maybe some ketchup?

No. Then, I would have to share.

I watched the small family and sighed. Sorry Reggan, but you would understand. You wouldn't leave them either. The smell of coffee hit my nose.

I miss my friend.

CHAPTER 20

Doc and his kids were asleep in the bedroom. I was slumped against the sofa, watching the flames dance around on the logs and thinking. I was so tired. Not just physically but mentally. Emotionally. I am so used to walking my own path. The whole me-against-the-world thing. Now, it appeared that most of the world and the aliens were against Reggan. A little old me, too.

She so needed me.

And I needed a better gun!

Think! Think! Think! Think! Think!

You know this area. We are at Ron's cabin.

Green's Bluff!

The small town was just down the hill. It wasn't that far. It was an hour hike. Okay, an hour and a half in the snow. Doc and his kids weren't dressed for the weather. Two hours. That was doable. I got them to the town. Then what? Maybe we will find more food and clothing. Then what?

Slow down, Ellie.

One step at a time. Get to Green's Bluff first.

I put another log on the fire and lay on the sofa with my shotgun. Finally, I couldn't fight any longer and closed my eyes.

I woke at first light, letting them sleep for another hour while I enjoyed three cups of coffee and two Kit Kat bars.

The breakfast of champions.

I woke them up and made them eat the last of the beans. Doc enjoyed the last of the coffee. I used my knife to turn some blankets into ponchos. I put plastic bags over their shoes. Then, I used duct tape to bind strips of blanket over their shoes and up to their knees. It was the best I could do. I did find some baseball caps. These would help keep them warm. You know, heat escapes through the top of your head.

We moved out in good spirits, but the cold soon dampened that. I had to keep dropping back to encourage them. Three hours later, we reached Green's Bluff. It really wasn't much of a town. A building that served as a combination gas station, post office, and quick shop for people going down the highway. There was a tiny hotel and a few other small businesses. The biggest place in town as the grocery/liqueur/ sporting goods store. It was a big green building in the middle of town. I took my small group over to the gas station. Once, I was sure that it was safe. Sadly, it had already been ransacked. "Stay here. I want to take a look around."

"The town looks empty," Bennett said.

"Looks can be deceiving," I said, moving toward the door.

"You going to be gone long?" Julie asked.

"No. It's not a very big town," I said with a smile and left. I made my way toward the store, thinking if there was anyone here, that would be. I crouched down and moved toward the broken glass doors. Actually, broken was an understatement. They were smashed to pieces. I peeked inside and was surprised. The shelves looked to still be full.

Why wasn't I happy about this?

I moved slowly into the store, moving up and down the front, peering down the aisles. Every shelf was filled, even the beer and liquor. All the rifles and pistols were gone. Why take the weapons and not the food? Maybe the owner sold out.

Maybe.

A cool chill ran down my back, and sweat beaded my forehead. Every nerve in my body was telling me to get out, but I just couldn't walk away from all this stuff. I picked one aisle and moved down. Each step took me into the darkness. It wasn't pitch black but dark enough to creep me out. Then it started to get light again. I came to the back of the store and froze.

There was a massive opening in the wall. It looked like something had ripped a hole in the cinder block wall. Some of the crushed concrete was still on the floor. There were some kind of animal prints I didn't recognize. I crept up and looked out. Fear swept over me as I took it all in.

There was a big hole in the ground right behind the store. It reminded me of a gopher hole, but this was huge. The gopher would have to be the size of an elephant. It wasn't just the hole that was scaring me. It was the big pile of bones piled up behind it. Human bones mixed with shredded remains of clothes. I knelt down and stared at the tracks in the snow. These were no tracks I had ever seen. Whatever it was appeared to have six legs, and there was more than one of these things.

Good times. Now, it looked like I had monsters to deal with. My luck just keeps rolling.

I glanced back at the hole. Then, I followed the wide trail around the store. The tracks out into the street moved right. Then, right down the middle of the street and back up into the mountains. What was really creepy was how straight the trail was. Good news. It looked like the creature and his buddies had left town. I stood up and looked back at the store. "Oh man, that is just too scary to think about."

Could these creatures have used this store as bait? Come in, stupid humans. Everything you need is right here. Come on in. I am starving, and you are just so tasty!

I stood there for a long time. Debating what to do.

"Ellie!"

I turned and looked back at Doc. He was standing there in that stupid poncho, with strips of cloth wrapped around his lower legs. Even from here, I could see he was cold. They wouldn't last long like this. I waved and yelled for him to come up.

CHAPTER 21

I stood at the back of the store, watching the big hole. I was pretty sure that whatever lived there was gone, but maybe not. Doc and his kids were putting on new snow gear. Julia was now wearing a bright pink snowsuit.

Pink. Not the best choice.

Ever try telling a six year old she can't wear the cute pink snowsuit? Pink it is.

I got bored watching the hole and wandered over to the sporting goods department. I checked the drawers and cupboards. I found three boxes of shotgun shells. Once these were stowed in my pack, I saw three backpacks. A big one for Doc and two small ones. I filled a cart with other camping gear they would need.

Oh, I picked up three bottles of ketchup and more Kit Kats. Doc and the kids came back with three shopping carts filled with food.

I sighed.

"Okay, we are trying to avoid the cans because they are too heavy. I'm not saying we can't take some, but not a lot. Anything that we can't cook in one or two pots is a no-go," I said. The kids looked disappointed. But chocolate is an excellent source of sugar. We need that. So chocolate bars are in."

That got some big smiles. The kids took off for the candy section. Doc rolled his eyes.

"What?" I asked. "You worried about cavities? Get a toothbrush. Getting fat? They will be working that candy off in no time. We're going to move across to the hotel. Get yourself packed, make some hot food, and rest. I'm thinking we might spend the night here."

"You sure," Bennett asked, looking back toward the hole. "I saw the hole and bones."

"The tracks leaving out of town. I think we are safe for now," I said, checking the carts and holding two cans of sloppy joe mix. "You got hamburger?"

"No." Doc said with a laugh. "Kids."

"We'll take one. I might be able to bag a rabbit or something."

"You are a nice person. You act tough, but you have a good heart. Before you came along, we bumped into a hunter and his three kids. I asked for help. One of the kids shot a bullet over Julie's head. The dad said it was a brave new world and that we should just lie down and die. People always surprise me, and not always in a good way."

"Hey, normally I would have left you. I am just doing what Reggan would have done. I couldn't look her in the face if I just ditched you. Come, let's get this stuff across the street."

Bennett smiled and shook his head like he didn't believe me. Maybe I should shoot him in the foot.

Just kidding.

CHAPTER 22

Julie and Jason stirred the stew and mixed it with spaghetti.

Kids.

I wasn't worried. I had my ketchup. Bennett was laying out the new sleeping bags. We were camping out on the second floor. I was at a window that overlooked the main street. I was thinking about the empty cans that we found in the room. Someone had been here and left. I flinched as two gunshots came from the nearby forest.

"Those were close by," I said, looking back. "I am going to take a quick look around. Stay here."

"You sure that is safe?" Bennett asked.

"No, but they could be friendly," I said, moving toward the door. "Save me some food."

The kids laughed. I wasn't fooling. Those two ate like horses.

I went downstairs and moved down the street, using the buildings and cars for cover. I came to the town's edge and listened.

Nothing.

But the hairs on the back of my neck were standing up. I moved across the main highway, crossed the train tracks, and into the woods. I was only a few feet in when I saw the tracks. I knelt down and studied them.

In case you haven't noticed, I am an expert tracker. We are talking sixteen-year-old Daniel Boone here. These tracks belonged to people wearing boots. Two, no three, possibility four. I needed to know who they were. You may find this surprising, but it is easier to stalk people than animals. Deer and such are always on their guard and moving slowly. Predators like bears and wolves creep along. You've seen movies or TV shows showing the wolves running through the woods, looking majestic. How many animals would wolves catch if they were charging through the woods? That's why deer have eyes on the sides of their head and big ears. So they can see and hear the things hunting them, including us. Animals only run when they are scared or being hunted.

I followed the tracks.

Slowly.

I stopped when I heard some yelling. It sounded like kids. There was a clearing just ahead. I crept up to a big tree and peeked around. There were three kids in the middle of the clearing. One was lying in the snow, looking like he was hurt. The other two were standing over him, yelling for help. They were saying he got attacked by a bear.

A bear?

I don't think so. Bears rarely attack people. I know you are thinking about that movie where the bear mauled the mountain man. He got between the bear and her cubs. That is a big no-no. Nine out of ten times, the bear doesn't want trouble. He wants food. You see a bear slowly back up, being as non-threatening as you can. Don't climb a tree. Bears can climb trees. Probably, better you.

I watched the kids and then remembered what Bennett had told me. Now, where is Daddy? On top of that, where was the blood? This kid was supposedly mauled by a bear, and there was no red blood on the white snow.

The word 'trap' came to mind.

I moved back down the trail and started to circle the clearing. Sure enough, I found Daddy's tracks. The guy wasn't even being careful.

But I was.

I followed the tracks like I was stalking a deer. A deer hears and smells a lot better than a man. I am no deer, but after a few seconds, the smell of tobacco hit my nose. Was this guy asking to be found? He might as well be yelling, "Here I am! Right behind this big tree."

I came around and spotted the guy. He was dressed completely in camo green with a matching cap. Mr. Hunter was kneeling beside a big oak, using it for cover. A cigarette was hanging out of his mouth. He probably carried a six-pack in the woods back in the day.

Moron.

There was a rifle with a scope resting on his knee.

Was that a Weatherby Vanguard? Be still, my heart. If I was really lucky, it would be a series 2.

Like I said, I needed a better gun. Trust me, this will do. The scope looked pretty sweet, too.

I crept up right behind the guy and pressed my shotgun right against the base of his neck. He froze and then gulped. His cigarette dropped into the snow when I pulled back both hammers. "Are you hunting wascally wabbits or me?"

"Don't shoot me. I am..."

"I have a pretty good idea what you're doing," I said, trying to sound cold as ice. I am pretty sure I hit the mark because the guy gulped again. "You are still holding that very nice hunting rifle, which tells me you are thinking about what to do. Now whatever you do next will be live-changing or life-ending."

The rifle dropped to the ground. I shoved the hunter forward into the snow and snatched up the rifle. Series 2! With a night scope! Score one for Ellie!

"Tell the kids to drop the guns and get on their knees," I snapped as I slung the rifle over my shoulder. The kids were dressed in camo too. Two were holding rifles. Probably 22's. Small, but they will kill you.

"Boys! Drop your guns and get on your knees. We got a situation here," the dad yelled, looking over his shoulder and trying to look mean. I glared back. He looked away. I must be improving on my Clint Eastward stare.

The kid lying down jumped up. All three aimed their weapons and yelled for me to drop my gun.

Really?

They were just as bright as Dad. I pulled Dad up and used him as a shield. I dropped the shotgun, laid the rifle on his shoulder, and whispered in his ear, "Don't even think about moving."

Another gulp, or was that a sob?

I took aim at the three kids.

No, I am not going to shoot kids.

One was wearing a cowboy hat. At this point, I should tell you that I am a pretty amazing shot. We are talking about Annie Oakley. I hope you know who I'm talking about. I focused, took a breath, held it, and squeezed.

The kid's cowboy hat flew right off his head.

Sweet. I am so good.

"You want to keep your heads? Drop the guns and get down in the snow," I yelled. Dad started to move, so I smacked him with the barrel as I jumped back. When I brought up my rifle, all three kids were face-down in the snow. I kicked the jerk. "All right, get up!"

He muttered a few words that I can't put on this page. They were, as people say, colorful. I told you I don't swear much. Kids look stupid swearing.

I marched Dad out to the kids and checked their weapons. Two were lever action Winchesters and not 22s. The last was a pump shotgun. Serious hardware. These guys looked to be twelve, maybe thirteen. This was too much firepower for them. "That is some serious weaponry you guys are packing. You sure you can handle it?"

"I should have shot you when I had the chance," one of the kids growled into the snow. I shot over his head, which produced loud screams. One started to sob. These guys needed to know I was in charge and not to be messed with. "One, you don't have scopes on those. Two, I have already demonstrated how good of a shot I am. Three, I can still shoot you. Four, you are a kid. Shut up! Now, where is your camp?"

"We don't have one," dad said too quickly and looked down.

"You are not packing food. I don't see packs," I growled. "I grew up around here. I hunted out here. Now, where is your camp?"

I shot two more bullets over the kid's head. The smallest one screamed and pointed west. "Thank you."

I switched to my new pump shotgun. The beauty of a shotgun is that you really don't have to aim. You squeeze and pump. I made the small kid carry the other to rifles. Then, the four of them marched in front of me. I heard whispers. Probably plotting their great escape.

As if.

I walked down a narrow trail until we came into a clearing with two tents. I ordered my prisoners to drop and looked around. I gasped. "Jersey?"

CHAPTER 23

I couldn't believe what I was seeing. There were three men bound and gagged with duct tape. A chain wrapped around their ankles was then locked around a tree. All three were stripped down to their Tee shirts and boxers. They all looked like they were not only freezing to death but looked half starved. One of them was New Jersey. The soldier that couldn't shoot from the camp. Then I noticed one of the guys had been shot in the shoulder. Some dirty rags had been wrapped around it. I was shocked and pissed. "What the hell!"

Sorry, I got very upset.

"ON YOUR FACES NOW! DO IT! EITHER ONE OF YOU MOVES I WILL KILL YOU!" I yelled, shoving Dad over with my boot and poking one of the kids with the gun. They all lay face down. One kid and Dad looked up. I fired a shot over their heads. "DON'T MESS WITH ME!"

They buried their faces in the snow. I moved over to Jersey and ripped the tape off his mouth.

"OW!" Jersey yelped and then laughed. "Ellie! I'm glad to see you. Its okay, boys. We are saved."

"What the heck is going on?" I said, pulling out my knife and cutting Jersey free. I handed him the knife, went over to Dad, and kicked him. "KEY!"

I know what you are thinking. Boy, Ellie, you are really being mean. Yes, I was. In my defense, it worked. Dad pulled a key from his pocket. I snatched it and pushed his face back down in the snow.

Yes, it was really hard, and I did mash it around. Just a little.

"Here," I said to Jersey, handing him the keys. I watched Dad and the boys while he freed himself and the others. They began to search the tent for clothes. Finding none, they stripped Dad and divided them up. They tossed a coin for the boots. Luckily for the kids, their stuff was too small. One of the guys started to make a fire. "Don't bother. I know a place close by where you can get all you need."

"Lead on, Ellie," Jersey said, wearing only a shirt, boxers and socks. "Oh, this is Wayne, and that's Kyle."

They both thanked me. I handed out the weapons. Jersey was given my double barrel shotgun after much debate. It turns out Jersey really was a terrible shot. With the four captives in front of us, I led them back to town. "You want to tell me what the heck is going on here?"

"They're bounty hunters," Jersey said with disgust. "The army is offering bounties for deserters."

"You guys deserted?" I asked, still keeping an eye on our captives and the woods. The world was becoming a crazy place.

"Yeah, I didn't join the Army to become an asshole or mindless robot. I don't shoot families," Wayne said, glaring at the three boys trudging ahead of us. He had lucked out and won the boots, so he wasn't shivering as bad as the others. "But these three are making me reconsider that position. The jerks would kick us and then eat right in front of us. Who's laughing now?"

Wayne kicked one in the butt and told him to move faster. He smiled when the kid yelped.

"I told you about Watershaw," Jersey said, moving beside me.

"I met the man. Talk about an asshole," I said, pointing the group across the tracks toward the town. "He actually expected me to betray my best friend. I opted to leave."

"Man, he was pissed," Jersey said with a laugh. "He ripped apart the camp looking for you. He couldn't accept the fact you had escaped. How did you get out?"

"Roof panels and a truck," I said with a big grin, happy that I had more than annoyed the general. "I hear there is a bounty on my head."

"Not as big as your buddy's, but big enough," Jersey said and stopped at the edge of the town. "You sure this place is safe? I passed by it a couple days ago. Bob went in to check it out and didn't come back."

"Yeah, it's safe," I said, moving to the head of the group. "The store has clothes and food. So, what is the deal with these guys? I know he was using the kids as bait. Is that how they got you?"

"Yeah, we walked right into that one," Wayne grunted, almost kicking the kid again. "We thought we were saving their butts. We walk up. Suddenly, the kids are pointing their guns at us. The old man shot me for no reason."

"So why are you guys deserting?" I asked.

"Watershaw had been bringing in his own men," Kyle said. He was a tall, skinny kid with a too-big nose and lips. He did have a sweet smile. "You probably seen the guys in black."

"Oh yeah, the puppy killers," I said.

"Puppy killers?' Wayne asked. He was short but stocky. Mostly, it was fat.

"Guys, who would shoot a puppy and brag about it later?" I said.

"That is a good name for them," Jersey said with sad laugh. "Watershaw is sending patrols to all the cities and towns in the area. Letting the people know he is in charge. We saw some of your puppy killers take out an entire family. We decided that Texas was sounding pretty good."

"They took away our weapons at night," Kyle said, which is why we were unarmed when these jerks got the jump on us. They were going to take us back, but when they heard Zero was in the area."

"Zero is what they are calling your friend," Jersey said. "I don't know if it is true or not. They say your friend has changed. You know, mutated."

"I have heard that, too," I said, motioning everyone into the store. I looked over at the hotel and whistled. Doc poked his head out a window. "We got company. One of them needs you."

The kids were edging away. I fired a shot over their heads. "Really?" They all began to cry. I rolled my eyes.

CHAPTER 24

"You're lucky," Bennett said as he bandaged Wayne's shoulder. "The bullet went all the way through. There is no sight of infection. I will give you a couple of penicillin tablets to be sure. I suggest we get some food into you guys."

"The kids are helping with that," I chuckled. "I hope you guys like beef stew with spaghetti-os. I recommend adding ketchup."

"I'll take anything right now," Kyle said, trying on a jacket and looking at his reflection in a mirror. He was wearing yellow ski pants, a red shirt, and boots. This guy was worried about how he looked. He nodded and smiled. "This works."

"Really? I have a friend named Trisha who would probably be throwing up right now," I said, glancing over at Dad and the boys. They were sitting on the floor with their hands and feet duct taped.

Yes. The kids, too. No, we are not going to kill them or torture them. The plan was to turn them loose when we left. Without weapons, of course. No way was I giving up this rifle.

"You guys have a plan?" I asked, glancing out the door. I know whatever left those tracks was gone. It didn't mean they wouldn't come back. Still, I was thinking we should hold up here for a couple of days or they should. I had to get to Mammoth. "I think you mentioned Texas?"

"Yeah, we hear that there are no aliens down there," Jersey said. He was dressed from head to toe in camo hunting gear and did not look like a hunter—more of a geek trying to look like a hunter. He was helping the kids with the food. They had a big pot resting on top of a camp stove. I watched as he dumped a can of beans and some spam he had cut up into the pot.

"What the heck are you making?" I asked, not sure I wanted to know.

"It's called Mulligan stew," Jersey said, stirring the pot. "Hobos used to make it back in the day. Basically, you put whatever you had into a pot and cooked it. It's smelling pretty good."

The kids laughed and clapped. Doc and I rolled our eyes. Wayne moved his shoulder around, thanked Doctor, and went in search of warmer clothes. Bennett moved up beside me and watched his kids. "We would be dead if it wasn't for you. You are not staying?"

"Come on, Doc. These guys can take care of you," I said, looking down. You have to go to Texas. You and the kids will be safe there. It's not safe to be around me. Once I hook up with Reggan, it's going to be even more dangerous."

"I hope you find Reggan," Doc said with a sad smile and squeezed my shoulder.

I muttered something and walked off to find some more candy bars. I found a whole box of Kit Kats.

Score one for the kid.

CHAPTER 25

I stood watching outside the hotel while everyone else got some shut-eye. I could use some sleep myself, but my brain was going a mile a minute. The moon looked bigger and brighter than I could ever remember it being. It was framed by billions of stars. It was really beautiful. The moonlight made the snow glisten. It looked like tiny diamonds were buried in the snow. My eyes were getting heavy, but I still needed a game plan. Mammoth was still the goal.

What if Reggan wasn't there? Then what? She could be heading for Texas, for all I knew. I told myself I just had to get to Mammoth. Then I could worry. I needed some sleep. I went back into the hotel and checked on our prisoners. They were all sleeping on the floor.

Hey, we gave them sleeping bags and pillows.

Jersey came down, holding his shotgun. He smiled. "I'll take over. Get some sleep."

"Thanks," I said and headed up the stairs.

"You're not coming to Texas, are you?" he asked, giving me that crooked grin.

"No. I got to find Reggan."

"Do you even know where she is?"

"I have a plan. Besides, that's my problem. Your problem is getting those kids to Texas. Who knows, they may have computers for you to work on."

"Come on, Ellie, You're a kid." I could tell he regretted saying it. "I mean, there are aliens out there and the p killers. You need someone to watch your back."

"Are you volunteering?" I laughed. "We have already established that you are a terrible shot. No offense. You wouldn't be much of a backup. Besides, I'm better off alone."

"I can see you are pretty tough and smart. You know your way around a gun and can survive in these woods better than I could ever hope to. You can probably rub sticks together and make fire."

"As a matter of fact, I can. It would be more of a challenge in this snow. Jersey, I appreciate the offer. I plan on moving fast. Mammoth is still a good ten miles in the snow. I am going cross-country. I won't have time to watch your butt. I'll be too busy watching mine. Besides, Reggan is probably there."

"You always been like this?" Jersey asked, studying my face. "I mean so...so...independent. Refusing help from anyone."

"Pretty much," I said, not feeling bad about it. "You got friends and family back in New Jersey?"

"I come from a big family," he said with a smile. I could tell he was thinking about them. "A lot of good friends. I miss them."

"I can count my friends on two hands. Most of those are just people I know. Reggan and Trisha. They are my best friends, and I would die for them. Once I hook up with Reggan, we'll go looking for Trisha, as for my family. Mom and Dad tried to get me to betray Reggan for a plane ticket to Texas. I don't blame them. They're scared. Everything they had is gone and probably won't be coming back. Even if we win this war. The world will never be the same."

"So that is a no on me going with you," he said, looking hurt. "You know I'm tougher than I look. I really think I could help you."

"Look, I am tired," I said, giving him a fake yawn. "Let me sleep on it."

"Deal."

CHAPTER 26

I left just as the sun was peeking over the mountains. I had stuffed my pack before lying down in a sleeping bag. I made a quick breakfast of fried spam sandwiches and coffee. I was on the road before anyone woke up. Jersey had fallen asleep on the sofa in the lobby.

If he was still in the Army, they would have shot him. I just gave him a pat on the head and left.

I am not big on goodbyes.

Jersey would probably whine about me not letting him come along. That was all I needed; a guy from New Jersey who couldn't shoot. He was better off going to Texas. I left the double barrel shotgun but took the pump and my new hunting rifle.

It would do until I found something better. I had a feeling that I would need an automatic weapon. Maybe- an M16 or an MP5. That would be sweet.

I decided to stay off the main road and cut across country. Luckily, it hadn't snowed again, so the snow was getting hard and easier to walk on. I kept my eyes on the ground for tracks. A lot of deer and some bears. I came out of the woods and found a backroad that I knew. It ran alongside a river. It wasn't a big river but was still too wide to jump across, and the ice looked iffy at best. I came to a wooden bridge, started across, and stopped. Something had put a big hole in the middle, like a shell from a cannon or bomb from a plane.

Thank you, God, for making it just a little harder.

I was tempted to jump across with the pack on my back, but that would be iffy, too. I could take off my pack and throw it across. While I was debating this, I saw another bridge upriver. It looked intact, but if it wasn't, I could come back.

I was trudging toward the bridge when I heard loud talking. I stopped and brought up the shotgun. A few moments later, seven people walked out of the woods and onto the road. They made no attempt to be quiet.

Morons.

There was a big guy in front wearing a mismatch of clothes. Sweaters and jackets were becoming a fashion statement. He was holding an old M-1 and had a Colt six-shooter jammed into his pants. Four other men were with him dressed similarly. Two teenagers were pulling what looked like a makeshift sled. A wooden box on steel rails that looked very heavy. Too heavy for the kids. The two boys were grunting as they pulled it. They were sweating, which is not a good thing in cold weather. The sled was filled with clothes, boots, and other junk. I didn't like the look of these guys, so I moved up a hill behind a tree and waited.

The guy in front raised his hand and yelled for everyone to stop. The two teenagers dropped to the ground. They were gasping for breath and didn't seem to mind the cold snow. He moved forward with his rifle ready. My finger wrapped around the finger of my trigger. He stopped by my tracks and studied them. A smile spread across his face. I knew he couldn't see me but could follow the tracks.

"Be my guest," I thought, pointing my barrel in his direction.

"I know you are up there," he yelled, standing up and looking into the woods. "I can tell by your tracks that you're small. You would be better off coming down and joining up with us. I'll take care of you."

Yeah, right.

I didn't say a word. I glanced back at the group. No one was moving. The other men held rifles but looked just as exhausted as the boys. It was then I spotted the chain. The two teenagers were chained to the sled.

I'm sorry, but I have no interest in being your mule. I readied myself, deciding I would take out the leader first. By the look of the other guys, I suspected a few shots over their heads would make them run. I was just debating whether to switch to my hunting rifle when I heard them.

Branches were breaking behind me. It sounded like bushes were just being crushed down. Whoever it was, they were moving fast. They were making no attempt to be quiet. The man down the hill yelled something, making me look down. Another crash and what sounded like clicking sounds. The sound scissors make when you click the blades together. I glanced over my shoulder and screamed.

Then I ran.

I ran past the big man down the slope and kept running for the bridge. He looked surprised when I ran by. It took him a second to realize what had happened. He yelled stop or he would shoot.

I looked back and yelled. "RUN!"

He was confused but must have heard them because he looked up toward the trees. A second later, they came out.

They were bugs. Not small bugs but about the size of a big dog. Long bodies with six legs and long claws out in front. The clicking sound came from these. Arched over their yellow and black bodies was a scorpion-like tail with a stinger. Their eyes were blood red. So was their bug-like mouth, complete with drool. They made a loud gurgling sound as they moved.

I kept running. I was focused on the bridge. More bugs came in front of me. Thank God the snow was deep. It slowed them down, but not by much. One was getting too close for comfort, so I aimed and shot. The blast made its buggy head explode. It dropped to the ground.

Good. The bugs can be killed.

I reached the bridge, pulled off my pack, and threw it across the gap in the bridge. Clicking made me whirl around. Three were scurrying up the bridge. I blasted away until the shotgun was empty and the bugs were dead. I began to reload while taking several steps back. Loud screams made me look down the road. The mutant insects had overrun the small group except for the big guy. They swarmed around the group just like I had seen ants do. Just like scorpions, they used their stingers.

It was pretty disgusting.

The big guy was running toward me. One of the other men broke free and followed him. He was making pretty good time until the big guy turned and shot him.

I watched in horror as the men and teens were ripped apart. They were gone in seconds. Then, the swarm moved toward me. I took a few deep breaths, ran, and jumped. I seemed to slow down as I sailed over the gap. For a second, I was sure I would fall into the river.

Then I landed with a grunt. I rolled onto my back and brought up the shotgun. The big man jumped and barely made it. He landed with a loud grunt and rolled away.

A second behind him were the bugs. One was sailing across the gap with its claws reaching out for me. I fired right into its ugly face. It exploded just like a bug should. Another came over. I took it out. More bugs were trying to cross the river, but I was right about the ice. It broke, and they sank.

Good riddance.

More bugs jumped, and I kept firing. I was still on my back. I used my feet to push me back as I fired. The shotgun clicked empty. I reloaded but only got six shells in before more bugs came. I kept blasting and pushing myself back. Once again, my shotgun clicked empty. I was panting and sweaty, thinking I was a dead girl. But there were only dead bugs in front of me. For some reason, the bugs had stopped jumping over. They just swarmed around across the bridge. They were debating what to do next or deciding if I was worth the effort. I am not that big. I froze when a barrel was pressed against my head.

"Just hand me the shotgun," he growled. "I need you alive."

"Shoot. I am not going to be your pack mule."

"Give me the gun!"

"Screw you! Shoot!"

"I am not kidding, bitch!" he yelled, reaching for my shotgun. My hand went down to the knife on my belt.

"Over here, jerk!" a voice yelled.

The big man looked back up and raised his hands, yelling at someone not to shoot. A second later, a loud blast filled the air. A double barrel shotgun was my guess. He flew back into the gap and into the river. I rolled over, ready to shoot, but didn't.

I couldn't. My shotgun was empty.

I looked up into the smiling face of New Jersey.

"See, I told you you would need me," he laughed, reloading his double-barrel shotgun.

"I stand corrected," I said, getting to my feet and looking back at the bugs. They were still just scrambling around like bugs, but I felt they were smarter than they looked. Could these have been the monsters from the store? If they were, I had been so lucky.

"I'm not the outdoor expert like you," Jersey said. "But I think we should get the heck out of here."

"Yeah. Quickly as possible," I said, pulling on my pack and looking back.

God, the world was really getting to be a dangerous place.

CHAPTER 27

Jersey and I made tracks away from the bridge and cut into the woods. I found a path probably made by a bear. It didn't look fresh, but I told my new partner to watch for bears.

"Are there really bears up here?" Jersey said, looking around as if a bear was about to emerge and attack.

"Not many bears in Jersey I am guessing," I said, moving up the path. "Stop worrying. It's not like the movies. Bears are more afraid of you. Unless they're really hungry or you get between a mother and her cubs."

"I saw that movie," Jersey said, still looking nervous. He followed me up the path. It was slow going but easier than I hoped. We came into some woods and followed another path. After a while, we came into a clearing and stopped. I told Jersey to wait while I looked around. It was a giant fir that had caught my eye. It might be an excellent place to camp. It looked like someone had the same idea. There was the remains of a small campfire. Maybe a few days old. They had set up a small camp stove. There was no sign they had camped here. It looked like they had just warmed up, eaten, and left. By the print of their boots, I estimated them to be tall but not heavy. The boots were new.

"What did you find?" Jersey said, walking over.

"Tracks. A couple days old," I said, thinking to myself. I was trying to remain calm. Tall and not very heavy.

Reggan? She was six feet in her socks.

If this was Reggan, she was going back toward Cornwall. I just knelt there, studying the print. Jersey cleared his throat, making me look up. "This could be Reggan. Probably not. I think we will camp here, but I want to look around. Stay put. Please listen to me this time."

"That works for me," Jersey said, pulling off his pack and slumping down against the tree.

"Good man," I said, pulling off my pack and handing him the pump. I checked my rifle and nodded. "I will be right back. Don't do anything until I do. Jersey, relax. The bears aren't going to eat you."

"You know I am almost twenty, and you are sixteen," he said.

"Your point?"

"Actually, now that I think about it, I don't have one. I did volunteer for this."

"Yes, you did," I said, patting his knee. "Have some water and a candy bar. That will cheer you up. When I get back, we will make something hot to eat."

I took off before he could reply. There was an excellent trail to follow, but fresh snow covered it. There were no tracks to follow, but something told me. Reggan had come this way. I needed to make a choice.

Which way should we go?

I forgot all this when I spotted a leg sticking out of the snow. Sadly, so had some other animal. It had been chewed on and looked pretty nasty. I crept closer and was thankful that the snow had covered up the rest of the guy's face and body. The snow around it was stained red. It looked like some kind of soldier, but what was left of his uniform was strange. It was more of a jumpsuit with padding. I suddenly had a thought. I began to dig around his body and found what I was looking for. A pistol. A Berretta nine. I thought the Army was replacing these. I dug some more and found clips for the pistol. I shoved the pistol into the back of my jacket and the clips into my jacket pocket. I had no intention of using it. God knows how long it had been sitting in the snow. I needed to clean and oil it. I spent another few minutes digging around for his rifle but came up empty. It was probably somewhere, but I didn't have the time to look. The sun was getting low. I moved on down the trail, keeping an eye for bears. Bears stayed close when they found a food source. The body was a food source.

I stepped into a clearing and stopped. This was the last thing I expected to see.

The wreck of a flying saucer sat in the middle of the clearing. It was mostly covered with snow, but it was definitely a flying saucer. It looked smaller than the ones I had seen on TV. Up close, it was not that impressive. Yes, it had taken damage, but it didn't look that...what is the word I am looking for...

Alien?

I moved closer, noticing the big jagged hole in one side. It had been hit with something. Once I was beside the thing, I realized the metal had been pushed out, as if something had exploded inside. I so wanted to go inside.

Alone? No, I had seen enough horror movies to know that was not a good idea.

I needed Jersey. Can't believe I thought that.

Then I saw the hand sticking out of the snow—not a six-finger alien hand, but a human hand. There was a man buried under the snow. Had he brought down the UFO and died fighting the aliens, there might have been aliens buried under the snow. I stood there like an idiot for a few minutes before my brain reminded me to get Jersey.

CHAPTER 28

"It looks kind of fake," Jersey said, standing beside the flying saucer. He reached out and touched it. "This feels like plain steel or something. You think it would be some alien metal. I read a book where a shiver runs through your body if you touch a UFO."

"Yeah, I read that too. Watch my back," I said, climbing into the opening and peeking in. "I am going to check it out."

"I want to see."

"You will," I said, rolling my eyes. "Let me see what there is to see first. Stay on your toes. There could be aliens around here."

"Like survivors?" he asked, nervously looking around.

"Yeah. Like survivors, but I doubt it. This thing has been here for a few days, at least," I said, looking around. I then climbed into the ship. I dropped down and found myself inside. The saucer just had one room. Two seats were mounted on the floor in front of what looked like a regular old control panel for a plane. There was no monitor, just a tiny and narrow windshield. Aside from some empty cabinets and a couple of counters built into the walls, it was very unimpressive. "I am so disappointed."

I moved around, taking in the interior, thinking this was a piece of crap. It looked like something one of those Star Trek or Star Wars nerds had put together in their backyard. "So disappointed. There is nothing cool about this ship."

"You okay?" Jersey yelled.

"NO! I AM DISAPPOINTED!" I yelled, hitting one of the walls, which shook. I kicked a few more times. "No way had this traveled through space! They made better flying saucers back in the fifties!"

I looked over when Jersey dropped down into the ship and looked around. I glared at him. "I told you to wait!"

"I heard you yelling," Jersey said, taking in the ship and frowning. "Wow, this is a piece of crap. It is not even airtight."

"Tell me about it," I growled, slumping into one of the two chairs and kicking the control panel. It shook, and dust fell as if to confirm the cheapness of this thing. "I was hoping for some cool alien stuff—maybe even some alien weaponry. But no! I get this, this. I don't even know what this is."

"It was made in the USA," Jersey said, looking under one of the counters. He pointed to some spray-painted letters on a panel. We made this."

"So much for pride in craftsmanship," I snorted. "I guess the army made this for some kind of secret mission."

"I don't think the Kapteynians would be fooled by this. You see any weapons or controls for weapons?"

"No, but I am not the expert," I muttered, thinking the only thing this ship was good for was shelter. It would be a good cover. My eyes caught something lying under the control panel. It looked like a plastic bag but looked like it had eyes. I got on my knees and pulled it out. It felt like rubber. I held it up and stared into the face of a Kapteynian. It was a mask of the alien, with bug eyes and big ears. It reminded me of those old Halloween masks you would pull over your head. "Jersey, look at this."

"What you got?" he asked, taking the mask and staring at it. Jersey studied it for a long time and then looked at me. "This doesn't make sense. Unless you are right about it being made for some secret mission. To do what?"

You will recall I told you I was a conspiracy buff. I took in the mask and the ship, then it hit me.

Or it could be my paranoia and my incredibly creative mind kicking in.

Suddenly I was pissed. It was like the gates of heaven opened, and I was all-knowing. "I knew it! I knew it! I was so right!"

"Right about what?" Jersey said, watching me stalk around the room and kick the wall several times.

I hate being right all the time.

"The one thing that had been bugging me was how easy the aliens pulled all this crap off," I said, turning to him. "The whole world goes to war, but not us. Aren't we always the first to jump in when the shooting starts and try to stop it? That's what America does. We did nothing. That is so unlike us. Why didn't we? Our government was working with the aliens. Don't you see? It all makes sense."

"Ah, paranoid much," Jersey said, shaking his head and looking over the ship. "There could be a good explanation for all this."

"Like what? Why would we go around pretending to be aliens?" I said. "I will bet my last dollar we got sold out by our president, congress, and corporate America."

"Ellie, you should calm down. You find a piece of crap ship and a rubber mask, and from this, you decide the people in charge are behind the alien invasion. Look around; we are fighting the aliens. This could have been made by someone else. Maybe it was so nerds..."

"Why? No, I am getting the big picture now. The plan is falling apart. Something happened to screw up the plan. I think the plan was for everyone to die except the select few."

"Why would they do that?"

"Come on, Jersey. The world was going down the toilet. We were polluting the Earth. Wars were being fought for the dumbest reasons. On top of that, there are just too many people on the planet. This world was not made to support billions of people. The problems were too big. Rather than work together and solve them, they decided to just start over. Clean planet. Clean slate. New world order. Was this the alien's plan, or did the boys in Washington develop this on their own? No. No. It was a joint venture."

"That's crazy. Our president didn't sell us out. The aliens showed up without notice."

"Did they? Roswell? Have you ever watched X-files or those cool shows on the History Channel? The truth is out there, buddy."

"Let's say for a second," Jersey said. He tried calming me down, but I wasn't buying it. Finally, I am vindicated. He put his hands up and said in a very calm voice. "You are right. What screwed up the plan?"

I looked at Jersey and had nothing.

"If you are right. The Aliens show up," Jersey said. "Then the President, Congress, or some blood-sucking CEOs make a deal. Maybe, just maybe, the aliens knew about the virus. They let us get infected. Start some wars to spread the virus. Everyone knows wars are great for spreading disease. Everyone was supposed to die in the war or by the virus. What had happened that messed up this plan? Why didn't everyone die?"

I looked at New Jersey with new respect. He was right. Something unexpected had happened. It had to be something right out of the blue. A light bulb went on in my head. I knew. It just popped into my head. I gave him a sad smile and said, "Reggan survived."

CHAPTER 29

"Geez, you are right," Jersey said, slumping onto the floor and looking into his lap as if the answer was too much. "Zero wasn't supposed to happen. Your friend was supposed to die along with the rest of us. Oh God, I am so stupid. Remember back at the camp? I told you I suspected they had the cure. They didn't give it to us until we started to grab our guns. I was doing a body count. Those guys back in Washington wanted to know how fast the virus worked. How long would it take to kill everyone?"

"I bet many powerful people sit nice, safe, and well-fed in big, cozy bunkers. Probably have cable!" I snarled, really feeling the need to shoot something or someone. A nice, fat, greedy slob of an oil CEO would be perfect. "Reggan survives. A local doctor comes up with the cure and gets a local company to make tons of it. This doctor thinks he is saving the world. He is just doing his job. It's too late; the guys back in Washington realize what's happening. They tried suppressing it, but word got out about the cure."

"It doesn't explain why we are fighting the aliens?' Jersey said, looking up. "Unless..."

"Unless what? What? What?"

"If you're the aliens, we suddenly devise a cure. They might just think..."

"We are double-crossing them," I said, giving him a big smile. "If the Kapteynians have been studying us. They would know we have a history of double-crossing each other. It is not a big stretch. We would double-cross them. Or it could be that aliens and humans have decided not to share. Would you want to live next door to the alien with creepy eyes and bat ears?"

"This is crazy. This can't be happening," Jersey said, looking up and looking very miserable. He rubbed his eyes and then scratched the top of his head. "That puts us in the middle. Which is a really crappy place to be."

"Jersey, I could be wrong," I said, moving over and sitting across from him. I took his hand and smiled into his gloomy face. "In the past, I have been known to get a little paranoid. Some people think I am crazy. Let's stop this and just get through the night. We'll have some dinner and coffee. Get some sleep, and in the morning, head out."

"And find Reggan."

"That's the plan."

"That's the plan."

CHAPTER 30

We spent a nice, cozy night in the fake flying saucer and headed out at first light. Actually, I spent a lot of the night fuming. It is one thing to suspect that politicians are evil and plotting against you. It's entirely another thing to find out you were right. In my mind, it explained so much.

Who is the crazy one now?

I tossed and turned in my sleeping bag. Finally, I gave up. I cleaned and oiled the Berretta. Now, I had an excellent pistol.

Thankfully, it didn't snow. The other good news was that Jersey was in a better mood. I even let him take the lead for a while. The trail was so obvious that my friend Trisha could have followed it. She is not a big outdoors person.

I needed to clear my head and think. It was all confusing. I was trying to figure out who the bad guys were. Who exactly was after Reggan? Was it the aliens, the army, or both? Were they working together? Why was it so frigging cold! Why did all the bad guys have better guns than me?

After a while, I took over the point and checked my compass. I really didn't need to. I knew exactly where we were. We were one, maybe two hours from Mammoth. We would be there by nightfall.

I was trudging along when a strange noise hit my ears. I motioned for Jersey to stop and kneel down. We both listened. The sounds made no sense to me. They were like a series of squeals, squawks, and chirps. Jersey moved right up beside me and whispered, "I think that it's aliens."

"Really?" I asked, giving my best 'you think?' face. Then I checked my shotgun.

"I heard them talk a couple of times," he said, looking around nervously.

Sarcasm is wasted on this man. I might have to switch to direct insults or just saying, 'Duh.'

"We are going to move up very slowly and quietly," I whispered into his ear. "Here, take the pump."

We exchanged weapons. I took the hunting rifle off my shoulder and clicked off the safety. I moved forward with both guns in my hands. We dropped down and crawled forward a few feet until we came to a fallen log. I peeked over. Jersey poked his head up, and I shoved it down.

Why was I letting him tag along?

In the middle of the clearing were about six aliens. These guys were new to me. They all stood at least seven feet tall. They had the same skin coloring, eyes, and ears. These aliens wore green jumpsuits with metal plates on them, along with silver helmets. Their big bat ears stuck out the sides. A visor covered the top of their faces, but you could still see the bug eyes. They were all holding strangely shaped weapons. The aliens seemed to be talking. No, arguing among themselves. The strange language started to get faster and louder. I was just about to crouch back down when another alien wearing a white robe with gold trim and a man dressed in black came out. Not black fatigues. He was wearing a black parka. I could see his shirt and tie under this, and he was wearing sunglasses. Wow, a real man in black. "Ah ha!"

"What?" Jersey said, poking his head up again. His mouth clamped close as he took in the small group. I could tell he spotted the man in black and scrunched his eyes. "Is he wearing street shoes?"

"That's what you notice? His shoes?" I asked, looking at him with disbelief. A low coughing came from the clearing, followed by loud yelling. Jersey and I looked back. One of the bigger aliens was coughing. The rest of the aliens backed away from him. A few of them raised their weapons. The man in black and the alien in the robe moved between them and the sick alien. I could hear the man yelling in an almost pleading voice.

"Wait! Wait. You have to stop this!" he said, raising his hands and looking into their bug eyes. "You can't keep shooting your brothers when they get sick. If he has got it, you probably all have it. Shooting him does no one any good."

"Jersey, the aliens really are sick," I said, not able to take my eyes off the group. The man was still asking them to calm down, and the aliens were all still yelling. The alien in the robes was talking in a calmer voice.

"Maybe they got some Earth virus like that old movie," he said, watching them.

"Yeah, yeah, the one with the Martians. You know, that was the first book by a famous writer. H.G. Wells helped create modern science-fiction."

"Really? I didn't know that."

I looked at him in disbelief when the word Zero hit my ear. My head whirled around. That got Jersey's attention, too. "Look. It is only a matter of time before we find the girl Zero. She is only seventeen. It is only a matter of time. Once we find her, she will give up because we have something she wants."

"What do they have that Zero wants?" Jersey asked.

"Don't call her Zero," I snapped. "Her name is Reggan. I don't know."

"Hey, it could be her mom or dad," Jersey said. "Watershaw is doing that. Grabbing family members, sticking them in camps, and keeping everyone in line."

"Yeah," I said, thinking who this creep had. I really wanted to talk to him. I was hoping he would leave alone. Then we could jump him. I was just thinking this through when a loud blast filled the air. Birds left the trees and flew away. Jersey and I watched red beams zoom into the clearing, removing all the aliens, including the sick one. Another group of aliens came into the clearing. They looked the same as the others, except their jumpsuits were dark blue. Their weapons looked much cooler. Sleek things with green lights blinking along the barrel.

Red laser beams shot out instead of bullets. The shooting stopped. The man in black and the robed alien were left standing in the middle of the bodies. They both raised their hands. I looked at Jersey. "Okay, I'm confused."

"You and me both," Jersey said as I took everything in. "Look!"

A whole new alien stepped into the clearing. This guy had to be at least eight feet tall. Not only was this guy tall, he was buff. I am talking some serious muscle. He was wearing a bright yellow shirt and black pants. The shirt had a series of colorful gems over one side of his chest. It reminded me of the ribbons officers in the military wore. There were purple gems on his shoulders that seemed to blink.

It reminded me of military officers who wear too many medals and ribbons. I always wondered, who are you trying to impress?

On top of that, he was wearing a cape. A black cape with yellow trim. He wasn't wearing a helmet but a small gold band around his forehead. His eyes and ears were bigger. A silver sword hung from a belt around his waist. A bigger and nastier-looking weapon was in his hands. The other aliens bowed as he walked up to the man in black, who seemed very nervous. This was obviously the alien in charge. I was so tempted to take the shot. One bang, and I could change the war.

No. Some other moron would just take his place. I was beginning to suspect there were just as many alien morons as there were human morons. Maybe the whole universe was just filled with morons. Perhaps the only clever thing these guys did was figure out how to travel through space. These guys were just like us. We showed up in America, and what is the first thing we do? Take over, and if anyone objects, kill them. Now that I think about it as a species. The human race is very disappointing.

"Well, this is new?" Jersey said. "Who is this guy?"

"If this was a movie, this would be Darth Vader," I said, counting and deciding there were too many to take out. They had cooler weapons. I am not being trigger-happy here. In my mind, all the answers to my questions were right in front of me. I was confident the big guy had all the answers. Maybe killing him would help end the war.

The man in black bowed slightly. The alien in the robe dropped to his knees and began to whimper in his alien tongue.

"Envoy, it is an honor," the man in black said. Then, he began to speak in the alien tongue.

"Don't," Envoy said in a deep voice that could have cut glass. What sounded like a growl came out before he spoke again. "Your tongue is not meant to speak our words. You speak of Zero. What do you know? Have you found her? Speak, Earthling."

"We are very close. We know where Zero is going," the man said, trying to sound braver than he was. Even from here, I could tell he was scared. We will get her. That is not the issue. The issue is you, and the Titan have to speak. This fighting is doing no one any good."

"It is eliminating your kind," Envoy said. "Your time in this world is over. It is our good fortune and the blessing of our gods that we found your world in time. A few more years, and you would have laid waste to it. And for what? That green paper has no real value. Yellow rocks and other pretty stones that you put such a high value on? You betrayed your own people. All the things you hold on to are mere illusions of power. I will show you what real power is by destroying all of you. Then I will make this planet the paradise it once was, and there will be peace."

"Don't get so high and mighty. You destroyed your world. That is why you are here," The man snapped, forgetting who he was talking to. The man in black seemed to remember and raised his hands to apologize. "Listen to me..."

The man in black never got to finish his sentence. The Envoy shot him. A green laser beam hit him. Then, he was engulfed in a green shimmering light. He screamed and was gone. Just like I have seen so many times in the movies. Jersey and I glanced at each other with big eyes. I smiled. "Cool, a real disintegration ray."

"Yeah, that's really cool. I think it's time to go," Jersey whispered into my ear. I could feel him shaking beside me.

"Right. We are outgunned here," I said, still staring at the ray gun and thinking I could really use that. I pushed the thought aside. I rolled over and stopped. Three aliens in blue stepped behind us. I looked up and smiled.

CHAPTER 31

They looked as surprised as we did. I brought the shotgun and fired both barrels. One of the aliens flew back into the bushes. A second later, Jersey was unloading his shotgun into the other two. The noise filled my ears, and gunpowder almost choked me. Both aliens flew back and vanished behind a fallen tree. Jersey and I glanced at each other and laughed until the laser beams started to fly over our heads. I grabbed his arm and pulled him along. "Run!"

"I'm coming!" Jersey said.

I was on my feet and stopped to try to grab one of the alien laser guns. Laser beams started to explode all around me. A green beam just missed me but hit one of the dead aliens. The body vanished.

I decided maybe not, and I ran.

I glanced back to make sure Jersey was following me. He was, but so were the aliens. Fortunately, they're not only big but clumsy. They kept tripping over branches and slipping in the snow. I couldn't see the big one. I guess chasing humans was beneath him. The path divided up ahead. I verged to the right, knowing this ledge went down. I was really moving. I glanced back.

No Jersey.

I stopped and brought up my rifle, using the scope to look for him. As I suspected, he had run left. Worse, he tripped. Three aliens were on top of him before he could get up. All three were taking aim. Without thinking, I took aim and fired. One of the aliens flew back into the snow. I worked the bolt and retook aim. The two aliens stood there like they were asking for it. I took them both out before they figured out what was happening. I lowered my rifle and yelled. "Jersey over here!"

This got Jersey's attention, and he waved. It also got the aliens' attention. Laser beams began to zoom all around me. I ducked and ran. I was so lucky these guys were terrible shots.

How were we losing this war?

I ran down the path that came out into the open. I ran across it, glancing back. No Aliens. Suddenly, the ground stopped.

Wrong turn.

I was standing at the edge of a high bluff, perfect for a sled or skiing. Sadly, I didn't have any skis or a sled. I was debating what to do when laser beams shot over my head.

These aliens really needed to put in some time at the firing range.

I pulled off my backpack, held it before me, and jumped. I landed halfway down the slope. My backpack acted like a sled. I was able to slide all the way down to the bottom. On any other day, this would have been fun. I came to a stop by a big rock and rolled behind it. Laser beams began to hit the snow and rock. I crawled under a fallen tree and brought up my rifle. There were four aliens at the top of the bluff. I squeezed my trigger, and one dropped. Another squeeze and another one down. The last two jumped back out of sight.

I guess they figured out the girl was a good shot.

A second later, the big guy stepped to the edge and looked down. I could tell he was looking for me. This guy was asking for it. I took aim but waited because he smiled and then seemed to laugh. He actually gave me a wave and then walked away. I should have taken the shot. On the other hand, he could have disintegrated me, the tree, and the rock.

Why hadn't he?

Maybe he decided I was a fellow warrior or something. I had taken out a bunch of his guys. I told myself he decided I was just too dangerous to chase.

That's right, I am bad.

I stayed behind the tree, thinking they could be setting a trap. A loud humming filled the air. I looked up when a flying saucer rose above the trees and hovered over them. It was spinning and glowing. This was the real deal. It hovered for a few moments and then flew off.

"All right, we will call it a draw," I yelled at the saucer. Next time, I will take you and all your bug-eyed buddies out."

I reloaded my rifle and the double barrel. Then, I went looking for Jersey.

CHAPTER 32

Backtracking to find Jersey was a pain. I had to make my way back up the hill, which meant I practically crawled up the stupid thing. My jacket was waterproof, not my jeans, so I wasn't happy when I reached the top. Putting aside my discomfort, I followed the tracks back through the path. I found some of the alien bodies.

Their weapons were gone.

"Thanks for nothing," I muttered as I stopped to search another alien body and found nothing. These guys really traveled light. Just their weapons and no alien food. I was really hoping to find some alien snacks. I was almost to the clearing when I heard voices. This made me crawl back up to the log. Soaking my jeans even more.

Not a happy camper at this point.

I peeked over the log. The alien bodies were still there, as were Jersey and another man in black. The man had Jersey on his knees, his hands behind his head. The man was standing over him, with his pistol almost pressing against his head. I was tempted to take him out, but I waited for a second.

"The girl you are traveling with. Is she one the called Zero?" he asked.

"I told you, man, I am traveling alone," Jersey said with a fake sob. He kept glancing around, spotted me, and gave me a look of 'What are you waiting for?' I gave him a 'just wait' sign with my hand. He didn't look happy. "I was just heading home when all the shooting started."

"You are lying," the man in black said. "Is the girl you're traveling called Zero? Does she have long red hair? She wears sunglasses all the time. This covers up her eyes. Listen to me, boy, she is infected with an alien virus. She is dangerous. She could have infected you. Luckily, we have the cure. So telling me what you know is in your best interest."

"I don't know anything. I am just trying to get home."

"Then you are useless to me," he snarled and took aim at Jersey.

Jersey looked right at me. Mr. Man in Black didn't even notice. Needless to say. This shot was a piece of cake. I sucked in my breath and squeezed. A second later, my bullet hit him in the elbow.

A perfect shot.

The pistol flew into the air and into the snow. The guy grabbed his wounded arm and dropped to the snow. He looked around as he reached into his jacket. I stood up and aimed. "I hit your arm because I wanted to. I can take it off your head if you like. Your choice."

He stared at me, thought about it, and dropped his good arm down to his side. Jersey jumped and found the pistol in the snow. Only then did he glare at me. "You sure took your time! I saw you behind the log. What were you waiting for?"

"Relax, you weren't in any danger. I am the one wearing wet jeans, risking hypothermia," I said, moving forward with my rifle ready. The man in black was glaring at me and shaking his head.

"You're not Zero," he growled.

"No, I am not, but I am an amazing shot," I said, smiling. "My name is Ellie. This is Jersey. And I have so many questions for you. For the record, her name is Reggan Sobe, not Zero. Let me tell you what we know. Our government is working with the aliens. Sold out the rest of us to save their own butts. So un-American. Abraham Lincoln, Thomas Jefferson, the Roosevelts, and Kennedy must all be spinning in their graves. Oh, thank you for confirming the men in black really do exist. Seriously, dress shoes in the snow?"

"I told you they were dress shoes," Jersey said with a smile. He was over being pissed at me. Then he poked the guy with the pistol. "From what we just saw, the plan isn't working out? Between you and me, I'm not surprised."

"No, it isn't. What was supposed to be a simple plan has turned into a huge mess," he growled again, shaking his head. Then he grimaced in pain. "Do you mind? I am bleeding here?"

"I don't mind. Do you mind, Jersey?"

"Well, since he was about to put a bullet in my head, I do not care at all."

"You don't have some clever alien device to stop the bleeding?" I asked, more as a joke than a question, but I was hoping he did. That would have been so cool.

"Contrary to what you have seen in the movies. We don't have a bunch of alien devices and weapons. Actually, our first contact was when they showed up. And that was by accident. Did you know they were wandering around up there for decades? It was a total fluke that they found our world. I hate to pop your bubble. Sadly, these aliens are not that bright and just like us."

"So when did you decide to sell out the rest of us?" I asked, wanting to rip those stupid sunglasses off.

"They appeared friendly at first," he said, rubbing his arm again. "The Kapteynians were actually starting to clean up the world. Of course, they had reached the same conclusion we reached years ago. There are just too many people in the world."

"So you decided to wipe us out?" Jersey yelled, almost pulling the trigger. "You..."

"Jersey! We need him alive," I said, putting my hand on the barrel of his pistol and pushing it down. I told you that I am pretty smart." Something in my brain clicked. "The original plan wasn't to wipe out America or Canada. Just the rest of the world. We would be the worker bees for the new order to build the new world. Was Canada in on it, too?"

"Here, I thought the Canadians were the nice guys in this world," Jersey said.

"You're right. The Canadians had no idea what the whole plan was," the man said with a chuckle. "The aliens gave us an antidote to put into the water system. No one was supposed to get sick. We should have moved on the Kapteynians the moment the virus started to spread over here. The aliens acted like they were surprised. Just as surprised as Cortez was when smallpox started to wipe out the Mayans."

"That was the Aztecs. Cortes was the Mayans. Read much?"

"Whatever. The bottom line is we knew the aliens were lying. Hell, we were lying. Everyone was lying. I wasn't there, but I heard the meeting got quite heated. The Envoy and The Titan were both there. Both acting all innocent. They gave us what they promised was the cure."

"Wait!" Jersey said. "You had the cure before her friend survived?"

"We thought we did. I told you, we put it in the water. We are not savages. People would be needed to rebuild the world. We even moved thousands to safe locations. Even some writers and artists. Some of your favorite actors and singers. A great many children. They are the future."

I couldn't believe this guy. He was talking like he was doing the world a favor. I saw the big picture. It wasn't about saving humanity. It was making sure the rich slobs and idiot politicians not only had servants but their cable TV and internet back in their new world order.

I am betting Taylor Swift wasn't in on this, but she could write a few songs about it. Then I realized that Taylor might be dead.

I almost shot him right then.

"The cure worked but not after it had been diluted in water. Only some people who got the undiluted cure survived. It looked like the aliens were going to win the game.

"Then the game changed again when my friend survived. You had a real cure. Which I am sure you gave to the New World Order but held back as long as you could."

"The Kapteynians didn't believe we came up with a cure by sheer luck. The cure would have been given out once we worked out an agreement. We were trying to avoid a war that would have lasted years."

"That's bull," Jersey said. "You were still deciding who would live and who would die. Still trying to create your new world."

"Let me guess," I said with a snort. "The President, Congress, and whoever are now in air-conditioned bunkers snacking on gourmet food and waiting for the smoke to clear."

"Some are in bunkers. Some on Hawaii and other islands," he said, groaning and glancing down at the snow that was turning red. "Actually, it was that doctor's fault. He didn't even contact Washington. He created the cure and took it upon himself to ship it out."

"Gee, I don't know why he did that?" I said in a mocking tone. "Maybe because everyone was dying, he cut through the red tape."

"The cure would have been given out in time. The aliens thought we were betraying them. That's when the Envoy started grumbling and asking why we needed the Earthlings. Fortunately, the Titan was calmer and more rational. We were just getting things worked out. Then the aliens started to get sick."

"From some Earth virus?" Jersey asked.

"No," he said. I noticed his hand moving toward his jacket pocket. I didn't say a word, but it did explain why this guy was so chatty. "The virus they brought with them mutated. That's what viruses do. They change, so they kill more people. In this case, the aliens. The aliens started to die."

I remember Bennett telling me the same thing about viruses.

"Now they are convinced that you double-crossed them," I said. "This Envoy guy makes his move. Now you have an even bigger war." My eyes were locked on his fingers. He was slowly slipping into his jacket. I could have said something, but I didn't. "That's why you guys want Reggan? You think you can get another cure off her. You get the cure and can make peace with the Envoy and Titan. Game plan back on track."

"Do you realize the mess this country is in?"

"You mean what is left of it?" Jersey snapped, almost shooting the guy again. This time, I didn't try to stop him. He didn't shoot but did kick some snow around.

"There is a giant mother ship orbiting our planet. We have yet to determine how many more aliens are up there. Right now, this country is divided right down the middle. The aliens hold the middle of this country. We have a good grip on the East Coast. The West Coast could be more stable. Canada has closed its borders and forced all the aliens out. Texas has declared itself a separate country. But the real battlefield is right here. The fate of the world hangs on your friend Zero."

"Her name is Reggan Sobe," I growled, almost smiling as his hand was in his pocket. Did he think I was blind and stupid? Then I had a thought. "Why not just let the virus run its course? Wipe out the aliens, problem solved."

Maybe not. Releasing smallpox on the Native Americans didn't work. They survived and were getting rich off their casinos until this all happened. Boy, those guys can't catch a break.

I knew the answer before he could reply.

"Oh man, you are still working with some of the aliens," I laughed. "The Titan? You need him. Could it be that soldiers actually dying in this stupid war are not robots? They are starting to figure out who the real bad guys are. You gave them the cure to buy time. But the seeds have been planted. Even if you take out all the aliens, the war ends. People will calm down and start to ask questions."

"Listen to me," he said in a very calm voice. Then, he made his move. The man in black pulled something silver out of his pocket and tried to bring it up.

I shot him.

Sorry. New World Order. New rules.

CHAPTER 33

I watched him fly back onto the snow and turned away. I staggered off a few feet and threw up. Hot tears ran down my face. Even after my stomach was empty, I still wanted to throw up. I stumbled over to a log and sat down. Jersey walked over, looking concerned. I pulled out my water bottle and drained it. It seemed to settle my stomach.

"You okay?" he asked. "The guy had it coming."

"It's not that," I said, taking a few deep breaths. "Well, it is. I mean, shooting aliens is one thing, but shooting us. That guy was a jerk, but he was still a human. He was one of us. It turns out all my conspiracy theories are turning out to be true. It is one thing to joke and laugh about evil politicians. Then to find out they're not only jerks but...puppy killers."

"Kind of sucks," he said, holding up a silver pen. "He had this in his hand."

"He was reaching for a pen?" I said, taking it and studying it. "He risked his life for a pen?"

I moved it closer to my face and found a small button on the side. I pressed it, and a thin silver needle popped up. "Wow, I am betting this pen doesn't have ink inside."

"Poison," Jersey said, shaking his head. "Careful with that."

"Oh, I will be very careful with it," I said, pressing the button. The needle slipped back in. I smiled at Jersey and slipped it into my pocket. "This may come in handy," I said.

"So what now?" he asked, looking around as if the world suddenly got too big. "This world is seriously screwed up. We are killing the aliens. The aliens are killing us and other aliens. Those morons in Washington are still trying to make their stupid plan work."

"And here we are stuck in the middle," I said, suddenly drained. Mammoth was close, but I didn't have the energy to move. I looked around and sighed. This was a crappy place to camp. There was no cover and no dry wood that I could see. We had no choice. "Well, Jersey, Mammoth is a little over an hour away. Let's get moving."

"Roger that," he said and put out his hand.

"Thanks," I said as he pulled me up. I adjusted my pack and nodded. We started to walk. "I saw him reaching for the pen. I could have stopped him. I didn't. I just wanted to kill him. Does that make me a monster?"

"No. Just human. You just beat me to it."

"Jersey, I am glad you are here."

CHAPTER 34

We didn't talk much. We were both in a bad mood. Finding out the world is going down the toilet and the people who were supposed to prevent this are behind it can change your whole attitude. We came over a bluff and stopped.

Sitting right in the path was another homemade sled, this one with more plywood and steel rails. Snow covered most of it, so it had been here a while. It was filled with boots, clothes, and other stuff. While I was looking for tracks, I spotted the boots sticking out of the snow. "I think I found the owner."

Jersey came over and looked down. He glanced back at the sled and shrugged. "I suspect he was up to no good. I found this under the tree over there. It's a clip."

"Actually, it is called a magazine," I say, taking the black magazine and studying it. "Didn't they teach you that in the Army? A small automatic weapon. Maybe an M-16 or MP5. Someone lucked out and got some serious firepower."

"I wouldn't mind some serious firepower myself," Jersey said, looking around and shivering. "Are we close? It's getting dark, and I am freezing my butt off here."

"Yeah, just down the hill," I said. "If we are lucky. We will soon be warm and toasty and eat hot food in no time."

"Yeah, we have been so lucky so far."

"We're alive."

"Good point."

We made our way down the hill. I caught a glimpse of a couple of bears, but they didn't seem that interested in us. Jersey spotted them and got really nervous. I was so tempted to make some bear jokes, but it had been a long day. A smile came to my lips when the tops of the buildings came into view. "There we go."

"Not much of a town," Jersey said.

"Bite me. It's a great town. I bagged my first ten-pointer here. There is a great river for fishing just over that hill. It's gone now, but there was a diner who made this amazing burger. Egg, bacon, grilled onions, and grilled tomatoes. It was the best. No Jersey, this was a great town."

"Maybe not that great," he said, stopping me and pointing down.

"This can't be good," I said, watching a long line of people being led out of town and over to a snowdrift. Four guys holding M-16 were urging them on. We ducked down and watched. It was then that I noticed some of the people in line were kids.

Puppy killers!

These guys were puppy killers!

Not on my watch.

"Jersey, take my..." I started to say but realized he still had my pump action shotgun. I let it pass. "Make your way down toward the back of that building. When I open up, they will make a run for it. You up for this?"

"Like you said, puppy killers," he said grimly and moved off. I made my way down to a tree and used it for cover. It was at this point some fat guy dressed in fatigues marched up. He was wearing a holster with a pearl-handled six-shooter. Two belts filled with shells crisscrossed his chest. He was holding an old-time Tommy gun, complete with the drum magazine.

This guy was a clown. I would take him down first, then the others. I put a bead on his head and was ready to squeeze when he started talking.

"I am so sorry about this, guys, but it is a new world," he yelled, not sounding the least bit sorry. About three dozen men, women, and kids kneeled in the snow. The women and kids looked terrified. The men looked pissed, and rightly so. "The old rules out. It is now the survival of the fittest. You guys are weak."

"Oh, you are so going down," I muttered, holding my breath and almost pulling the trigger.

"I mean, you let that red-haired girl just waltz out of here with a ton of stuff. She took an MP5! That was a weapon we could have used. No, the boys and I need to think about our future. This means hard choices."

"Reggan," I said under my breath. I needed Fatso alive. I moved my scope over to one of the guys taking aim with his M16. He had a slight smile on his face. I squeezed the trigger.

No more smile.

One of the other guys looked around and yelled sniper. I took him out. The other two guys started to fire into the air. Who were they shooting at? Morons. I put them out of their misery. Fat Boy started to run. He got about ten steps before Jersey jumped out and fired a blast over his head. The jerk dropped his gun and threw up his hands. My man, Jersey, walked right up and punched him in the face.

You go, Jersey.

CHAPTER 35

I made my way down to the people still kneeling in the snow. I could see some people still crying. For some reason, I got mad and was about to tell them to get up. Luckily, I realized they were just scared. I was going to pull out some candy bars for the kids.

"Ellie?"

I looked down the line of people and spotted an older man with black hair and blue eyes. A smile came to my lips. He smiled back. It was a smile I knew. I had hunted with this man. More than that, he was always friendly to me and quick with a joke. "Mr. Flemings?"

"Four for four," he laughed, getting to his feet and brushing the snow off his jeans. "I should have known. Not many people can shoot like that. I am glad you showed up."

"Me too," I said, helping some of the kids up and telling them everything was going to be fine. Well, as fine as it could be in this crazy world. "I would ask what was going on, but Jersey and I have already seen a lot of crazy lately."

Jersey walked up, shoving the fat guy. He was smiling. The six-shooter was pushed into the front of his pants. The Tommy gun was slung over his shoulder. "I didn't kill him because I heard him mention Reggan."

"Good man," I said, looking over at the man who had actually peed his pants. "You had an accident there? It's so embarrassing. Now tell me about the red-haired girl. Her name was Reggan, and I am looking for her."

"That was Reggan?" Flemings said as he helped more of his people onto their feet. "I thought I recognized her. I never hunted with her."

"Reggan never hunted. She just tagged along," I said, feeling good for the first time in days. "I remember one time she had this sweet deer in her sights. Couldn't squeeze the trigger. She fired a shot over its head and happily watched it run off. Probably thought it was Bambi's mom.

You know what? I wasn't even mad about it. That was just so Reggan. What the heck is going on here?"

"Well, you know about the bunker in Bart's," Flemings said, picking up the M-16 and pointing it at the fat boy. "I will be getting back to you, Harry. Mac, George! Chain old Harry up in the store. Give him a blanket and some water."

Two big young men dressed in army fatigues and holding two M-16s walked over. They shoved Harry toward one of the small buildings. A couple of kids hit the fat man with some snowballs. He didn't say a word.

"The deal was," he said, "You put some bucks in. We stock up on supplies and have someplace to run to. The end of the world took us all by surprise. Then the snowstorm hit us. God, you ever seen snow like this?"

"Just our luck for global warming and the alien invasion to happen simultaneously," I said, looking around the snow-covered buildings. A few kids were having a snowball fight while two smaller ones were building a snowman. Except for the men watching with guns, it could have been a Hallmark moment.

"You think that's what it is?" he said. "Maybe or maybe God is just pissed off at us. Your friend Reggan got here before us. I figure she got in just after the first big storm. She got everything she needed. An MP5, sniper's rifle, and a sawed-off pump. I am a little annoyed about that. I customized that for myself."

"So she left," I said, letting off a deep sigh.

"A little over two weeks ago," he said. "Reggan really put Harry in his place. She was locked inside nice and warm with lots of food and weapons. We were freezing our butts off and hungry. I figured that she must be family to one of our members. I told her we would back off and let her go. Not Harry. He bitched and moaned. We all went up the street to give her some space. It was too late, and I noticed Harry was not with us. Then we all hear a couple flash grenades go off. A second later some smoke bombs land in the street and she comes running like the devil. Man, she could move. Not just fast, but agile. Knocked Harry on his ass. He comes running out, but she was long gone by then."

"So you have no idea where she is going?" I moaned, feeling like the world's weight was back on my shoulders. I had a pretty good idea where Reggan was going—back to the place I had just come from.

"She is looking for her mother," Flemings said, watching Jersey fool around with the Tommy gun. He laughed and shook his head. "You are welcome to take that thing, but I warn you, my friend. It jumps around like a jackhammer and kicks like a mule."

"I like it. It feels good," Jersey said, holding the gun close to his chest. I almost expected him to kiss the stupid thing. Boys and their toys.

"Well, Jersey, you won't miss with that thing," I said. "Just make sure I am behind you when you fire that thing.

This got a laugh from Flemings and a few of the people who had walked up. They all thanked me, and I smiled and nodded my head.

"Really? Am I going to hear about my terrible shooting ability for the rest of this war?"

"My guess? Yes," I said, racking my brain for some kind of plan. People were taking my hand and shaking it. There were more pats on the back, and two ladies hugged me. I should tell you. I am not a big hugger and really don't like my personal space invaded. Jersey was trying to figure out the best way to fire the Tommy gun. I got annoyed. "I want to work with you if you want to take that thing."

"Can I have the six-gun too?" Jersey asked.

"I got a Mad Max on my hands," I said. Flemings and I laughed, along with everyone else. Jersey looked hurt at first but then laughed, too. "Harry here gets humiliated by my best friend and decides to take over."

"I have a feeling he and his dead friends were plotting from the start. I never liked him much. Didn't trust him at all. To be honest, you put in more money than he did," Flemings said. "More of our members have been showing up. Looks like things are getting bad in Oregon. He was bitching about that, too. Not stuff enough to go around. We don't have enough cots. Pretty soon, we will have nothing. These men and women paid and helped build this place. They were entitled to whatever we got. So that was Reggan. Her grandfather was the brains behind it. Did a lot of the work himself."

"Did his idea about the solar panels work?" I asked, remembering my talks with the old guy. I sure missed him. Then it hit me again. He was dead.

"He won't be showing up to enjoy all this," I said.

"I had a feeling he was dead," Fleming said. "Now that I think about it. I never mourned the guy. We will do something tonight. And yes, the panels work. We got power. If you are going after your friend, you will need to know a few things."

"Are you talking about our government selling us out or that some nut named Watershaw is trying to take over."

"Don't forget the Envoy and the Titan," Jersey said, still fooling around with the Tommy gun. He stopped and shivered. "Ok, I hate to be the greedy slob here, but there was talk of getting warm and having hot food."

"It seems you may know more than us," Flemings said, shaking his head. Come on in. We'll get you warmed and fed. You can even have a hot shower if you want."

"A hot shower," I said, letting off a low moan. The idea of hot water spraying over my dirty and aching body sounded like heaven. Yeah, I could relax.

Just a while.

CHAPTER 36

I was showered and shampooed. After this, I decided to trade up on my wardrobe. I was now dressed in my new cool clothes that promised to keep me warm and dry. My boots were fur-lined and waterproofed. My outfit was white. The matching jacket with a hood was slung over the back of my chair. I was also wearing new thermals. Mr. Flemings had told us to take what we needed. I thanked him but asked if we could eat first. The smell of something delicious had hit my nose.

Me and Jersey, who were wearing the same white outfit, were sitting at a table that had been set up. Flemings, along with several other people, were seated with us. We were both wolfing down beet stew and homemade biscuits. Between bites, I was telling them everything we had learned. The plastic mask was being passed around. More than a few curses and more people like me said it didn't surprise them that our leaders had sold us out. Remember, these people were preppers. They had little trust in the government before the war, and now their worst fears have been confirmed.

"God, I am not sure knowing had made me any happier," Flemings said, shaking his head and finishing his coffee. He offered me a refill, which I happily took. Jersey had drunk a couple of cups of coffee and was working on a root beer bottle. "I hate to say it, but it looks like Texas is the place to go. We could try to sneak into Canada, but I have heard rumors that they are shooting anything that tries to cross the border."

This made me laugh. I remembered telling Reggan that Canadians were shooting everyone, including dogs and cats. We both laughed about it. That was the last time we had laughed together. She had gotten sick not ten minutes later. I remember holding her in my arms and telling her she would be fine. Then I got sad.

I missed my friend.

Later in the evening, when most everyone had sacked out, I called Jersey to a small table in the corner. I had made some hot chocolate. We even had cookies. Store-bought, but any chocolate chip in a storm will do. "Jersey, I am going to rest up here for a day, maybe two. Then, I am heading back to Cornwall. That's where Reggan is going."

"I figured that would be the plan," Jersey said, dipping a cookie into his drink and shoving the whole thing into his mouth. "You need to check me out on the Tommy gun. I noticed some grenades back there. We may want to consider taking some of those."

"Jersey, listen to me. I am talking about going back into the lion's den here," I snapped, stopping him from taking another cookie. "Don't you get it? Me and Reggan are like lightning rods. The army and the aliens are looking for us. Watershaw is back in Cornwall. The odds are I won't even make it back to Cornwall. I will probably end up dead or captured. The army will probably shoot you for just being with me."

"I'm a deserter. They shoot you for that, too," he said, pushing my hand off his and taking another cookie. He dipped and ate it. Then smiled at me like I was some foolish kid. "I thought we had this settled. Yeah, it is dangerous around you. It's dangerous everywhere. Listen. You know, one of the reasons I joined the army was that I had no one. No family. I lied to you about having a big family. I don't know why. My dad and mom died in a car crash a couple of years back. Thank God they didn't live to see this. I was in a foster home until I was eighteen. Joined up. It wasn't what I expected. Nothing like the movies or the ads on TV. I didn't get the whole marching thing, and the food was awful. Not to mention, my sergeant had an obsession with clean shoes."

"The aliens showing up didn't help," I said, dunking my cookie and eating it.

"Actually, that made it a little better. Less marching, and no one cared about my shoes. Suddenly, I was in an office. Running numbers for them until I got sent to the compound. I wasn't here an hour before I heard about you. The dumb blonde who is plotting her escape. There was even a pool. No one thought you would pull it off. Without even meeting you, I knew you were smart. Then I got to talk to you. I told them to be careful. She's smart and pretty cool."

"Trust me. The adjective cool was never used to describe me in high school. Crazy. Weird. Remind me to tell you about the Vegan War I had with my parents."

"I saw your parents." He took another cookie but didn't eat it. He looked up at the ceiling like he was trying to remember something. "People really do strange things when they are afraid. They cried when they found out you escaped. I laughed my head off. Everyone was shocked. Watershaw took it out on everyone. Oh man, did I tell you? Your parents hooked up with some people going to Texas?"

"No. Didn't it occur to you to mention that to me until now?" I said, a little annoyed but hoping Mom and Dad were safe. It bothered me that I hadn't given them much thought until now. Yeah, they were jerks, but not all the time. Most parents were jerks at one time or another. It didn't mean I didn't love them. Maybe I should be looking for them. Then I remembered they tried to convince me to betray Reggan. What if they hadn't been so afraid? Where would I be now? I do tend to overreact. No. I knew my parents were safe. Reggan wasn't. Reggan needed me. Everything inside of me screamed that. "Forget it. Hey, you're not about to tell me you love me or something stupid like that?"

"You're sixteen," Jersey said, looking really shocked.

"I had to check. I am a blonde and pretty hot."

"You done? I'm being serious here."

"Sorry."

"Next time I saw you, you were saving my life. We hooked up again. I saved your life."

"If we are keeping track. I saved your life a few miles back," I said, dipping my cookie and eating it. "You will follow me even if I tell you not to."

"Yes. We are a team. On top of that. If I am with you, there is less chance of getting eaten by a bear."

"We have wolves here, too."

"You do not."

"They were almost extinct, but now, thanks to some laws and wolf-lovers, they are back. They probably love this cold weather. They hunt in packs and are really smart. There is a good chance Polar Bears had wandered down this far.

"Now you are lying."

"Polar ice cap is melting. Polar Bears got to go somewhere. One of the planet's largest carnivores, they eat anything."

"It's not enough for you that we have aliens, the army, and who knows how many more crazies out there. You have to add polar bears to the mix."

"Just keeping it real, Jersey. Just keeping it real," I said and squeezed his hand. "Oh, you forgot the mutant insects."

"Thanks for the reminder. Having a mutant cockroach eat me would be just my luck."

"Relax, I've got your back. Get some sack time. I'm going to start looking for gear."

"Tommy gun lessons in the morning?" he asked.

"Tommy gun lessons in the morning," I said. We clicked cups and drank, having no idea what we were walking into. Then I remembered something: "Jersey. I just realized something. I had a birthday. I'm seventeen."

"Happy birthday," he said and walked off.

CHAPTER 37

We ended up getting stuck in Mammoth for a whole week. Another blizzard hit us, and there was nothing to do but watch the snow fall and check out our gear. I managed to spend some time with Jersey and his new toy. He got the hang of it pretty quick. I took some turns with it but opted for an MP5. If it was good enough for Reggan, it was good enough for me.

On the day we finally left, it was clear and sunny but still cold. I decided to hike straight down Highway 99, reasoning that the snow in the mountains would be really deep. This plan worked for two hours, but then the war caught up with us.

Jersey and I were walking down the road when some aliens and soldiers decided this was the perfect place to fight the war. One second, we were just strolling along. The next second, bullets were flying all around. Followed by several explosions. The aliens came out charging from one side of the tracks. Then our soldiers came out the other side. They were both screaming like madmen. Jersey and I managed to duck into the ravine behind the train tracks. We crawled along while the battle raged around us. By some miracle, we made it up into the woods. We huddled down behind some trees and watched the battle. It really didn't last that long. Just ended. Real quick. Suddenly, the shooting stopped. The smoke cleared. The aliens lost.

No big surprise. They were terrible shots.

We watched the soldiers stand or walk around the bodies of humans and aliens. They stripped both, which struck me as kind of creepy. Jersey said that was a standing order. He reminded me we were cut off from the East Coast.

We made our way back to the mountains. This was harder and colder but somewhat safer. We still ran into battles here and there. The war had really come to Oregon. I took every chance I could to point out bears to Jersey. Which he didn't seem to appreciate. I kept praying to hear some wolf howls.

No luck.

We did come across some campsites. One person traveling toward Cornwall—I was sure it was Reggan—kept having to backtrack because of the war. Like us, she found herself running a few times because the army or the aliens would spot us. By sheer luck and some skill on my part, we escaped.

One morning, we were getting ready to move out. I figured we were close to Cornwall. We could get there by nightfall. If I was right, Reggan would go by and check out her house. I would. Jersey went into the woods to find a friendly tree. He should get his bladder checked. Fourth time today. Oh yeah, no doctors. When I heard the boots, I had just laid down my weapons to close my pack. My hand went down my MP5.

"Don't do it, honey! There are five rifles on you!"

CHAPTER 38

I muttered a few words that would have made you blush as I raised my hands over my head and turned. Five huge guys in black stood behind me with raised rifles. They were all holding SCARs. That is the weapon of choice for Special Forces guys. These had all the bells and whistles. Silencers, night scopes, even a grenade launcher. I was definitely outgunned here. They all had black ski masks pulled down, so I could only see their dark eyes. I didn't need to see their faces to know what they were.

Puppy killers.

I gritted my teeth when Jersey was shoved forward, landing just behind me. These jerks made jokes about his Tommy gun and six-shooters while someone called for Tango Man. I didn't say a word as they took the Glock that replaced the Berretta with my pack. After this, they just waited until a big man dressed in black walked into the clearing. He pulled off his ski mask, revealing a square face and buzz cut. His eyes shone but not in a happy way. I was guessing this was Tango Man. He had captain bars on his shoulders.

Good for him.

"What are you doing in this area?" he snarled, moving closer. He had forgotten to use mouthwash this morning, if he had ever used it.

"Minding my own business," I said, as cool as possible. I even gave the creep a smile. Which he didn't like. His smile vanished, and then he slapped me. It hurt like hell, but I would be dammed if I was going to cry or even shed a tear for this puppy killer. He asked me again. "Why don't you just slap me again? It's going to be the same answer."

Tango Man lifted his hand, and I braced myself for the hit.

"STOP IT!"

Tango man looked over his shoulder. He seemed very annoyed. I guess when he wasn't killing puppies, he was slapping kids around. He looked back and smiled. "Pretty tough."

"Give me back my weapons and a five-minute start," I said with a big smile. I will show you how tough I am."

The other puppy killers all laughed, but not him. One of the soldiers coughed. Tango Man suddenly straightened up. A tall, slender woman dressed in fashionable snow gear, complete with what I guessed to be a real mink coat, walked up.

PETA isn't around to stop her.

Behind her came an older man dressed in a suit with a too-thin snow jacket over it. He was wearing those rubber boots you pull over your shoes. I could tell he was freezing his butt off. Both of them stopped in front of me. The lady gave me a smile. It wasn't a genuine smile. It was a smile she practiced in front of the mirror. She practiced to impress people. I wasn't impressed. I did wonder who she was. The puppy killers seemed to be afraid of her.

"What's your name, sweetheart?" she asked, still smiling.

"Bite me," I said. Did she think the smile and calling me sweetheart was really going to make me spill my guts? I will give her credit. My clever retort didn't bother her.

"You do have an attitude," she said, pulling down my hood and yanking off my snowcap. My long blonde hair fell down around my face. The lady studied me for a moment. "You have to be Ellie. We have been looking all over for you."

"This is Ellie?" Tango Man said, looking at me with genuine surprise. "This is the one who escaped the camp and killed all those soldiers and aliens?"

"I am sure the number has been exaggerated," she said with a smile. "I do know she killed some aliens and a couple men in black. No great loss there. Oh, where are my manners? I am Darlene Chambers. The President's Chief of Staff. I have been sent out here to try and get control of the situation."

"If that is supposed to impress me, it doesn't," I said, looking over at Jersey, who they had pulled up. Two of the puppy killers were holding him in between them. These guys were acting like he was the biggest threat.

Big mistake.

"How much do you know?" Chambers asked, still smiling. I wanted to take a swing at her and give her dentist some more work.

I debated on what to say and decided to throw the dice. "I know the aliens showed up here by accident. I know El Presidente, with your help, sold out the human race. Actually, that isn't fair. You just sold out the rest of the world. If the virus hadn't come along, my friend Reggan wouldn't have survived. You might have gotten away with it. But now you got one big mess. You're still trying to make everyone happy. Good luck with that. The Envoy just wants to wipe all of us humans out. Not sure what the Titan is up to. My guess is it won't be good for people like me. You know, the real humans. Then you got that nutcase Watershaw. The bottom line is you need Reggan to fix things. You just can't find her."

"How? How? How?" The guy in the suit said. His lips were actually flapping. "How do you know all this?"

"Shut up, Sherman. You're looking foolish," Chambers said, giving him an icy stare and returning her attention to me. "Good help is so hard to find these days. Most of my staff was killed by the virus. Like you, I have a bone to pick with the aliens. You are right about Watershaw, but he is a necessary evil right now. He is bringing some stability to the area. We will deal with him when his services are no longer needed. Right now, I need you to help me find Zero."

"Her name is Reggan Sobe, and bite me again."

"Honey, I really don't need you," she said, this time with real ice in her throat. "I have your friend's mommy. I just need to get close to Zero—pardon me, Reggan—so she can realize surrendering is her only option."

"I don't think Reggan wants to be stuck in a cage and poked with needles," I said.

"Listen. It is more than a cure that we want from your friend. The virus has changed her. I'm not into some mutant alien monster that is killing everyone. It has enhanced her. Apparently, all her senses have been heightened. There have been unconfirmed reports that she is stronger and faster."

"I think I saw this movie. It never ends well for the person in the cage being tested. It always..." I said, then the light bulb went off in my head. God, I am so dumb. It wasn't about getting a cure. "Oh man, you never intended to keep the deal with the aliens. Once everyone was dead, you planned to kill the aliens. The virus changed everything."

"Yes, it did," Chambers said with a small smile. "Then Reggan's survival changed the game again. The aliens getting sick changed it again. The Envoy going rogue changed the game. Apparently, something called the sleepers could really change the game. No more! From now on, we have to get ahead of the game. This madness has to stop."

"Oh man, I have seen this movie. You want Reggan to help you create some kind of super soldier," I said, shaking my head. I was about to tell the President's Chief of Staff where she could go in colorful detail when a soldier ran up to Tango Man and whispered something. He nodded and smiled. "Miss Chambers, we have a confirmed sighting."

"Where?" Chambers asked, turning around and looking very anxious.

"She is back in Cornwall."

"Excellent. Do we have teams close by?"

"Yes, but so do the other guys," Tango said. "We are also getting reports of heightened alien presence in the area. They might know she is here."

"I want her! No more mistakes! This is a seventeen-year-old teenager. We should have had her weeks ago," Chambers said, turning back to me. "Put them on ice for now, but keep them separated. No, no second thought, kill the deserter."

"Hey bitch!" I yelled, moving forward, ready to give her a good smack in the face. I got shoved to the ground by Tango Man. Chambers was already walking away with most of the puppy killers. Tango Man told the others to take me as he pulled out his pistol. They were reaching down for me to drag me off.

CHAPTER 39

They were trying to pull me up, but I was kicking and screaming. Tango Man was pulling Jersey away. Then I remembered something and shoved my hand into my pocket. One of the creeps grabbed my arm. I pulled out the pen, pressed the needle, and jammed it into his hand.

"What the hell!" he yelled, jumping back and grabbing his hand. A second later, he started to shiver and gasp. Then he dropped to the ground, looking so very surprised.

The other guy looked over, trying to figure out what had happened. I jammed the needle into his leg. He yelped and looked down at me. A second later, he was on the ground. I rolled over. I looked for their weapons, but they only had the puppy killer's pistols and Jersey's Tommy gun.

That would work.

I shoved the pistols into my belt, picked up the Tommy gun, and ran in the direction that Tango had taken Jersey. I came around a tree. Jersey was on the ground, and the creep was aiming his pistol. He was actually taunting my friend. This guy was not only a puppy killer but a sadistic creep. "Jersey, get down! Hey, Puppy killer!"

Tango whirled around and froze. The look on his face was shocked, and then he smiled like he didn't have a problem in the world. A second later, he noticed the Tommy gun in my hands. The smile vanished as he brought up his pistol. I squeezed the trigger. The Tommy gun leaped to life, sending out a spray of bullets. For the record, it bucked like a bronco, but I held on tight. Every one of my bullets hit Tango Man in the chest. He flew back into the snow, landing with his hands and arms spread out. I ran up and looked down at him. He was still alive and looking shocked. "I told you I was tough."

Jersey got up and moved beside me. I looked at him and smiled. "That's three times I saved your butt. I am not sure if you are worth the effort anymore."

"Bite me," he said, taking one of the pistols from my belt and cocking it. "Come on, we've got some butt to kick and your friend to save."

"Roger that."

We ran off in the direction that Chambers had gone. It was a winding path that I knew ended in a clearing. We slowed when we came into the clearing. Then stopped, taking it all in. It looked like a mini-camp with tents that were being taken down. Supplies were being loaded into four trucks. They were all too busy to notice us. There were a couple dozen puppy killers, two trucks, and a jeep. On the far side were two helicopters coming in for a landing. I spotted Chambers and Sherman rushing to the choppers. Two puppy killers walked up and grabbed some boxes. They stopped and looked over. They dropped the boxes and tried to bring up their weapons. I squeezed the trigger. Then, I yelled for Jersey to get their weapons. He ran over and picked up one of the SCARs. I ran up and switched guns with him. "I am going after Chambers! Cover me!"

"I have so been waiting to use my baby!" Jersey said, bringing up the Tommy gun. He braced himself and opened up. He sprayed bullets all across the clearing. Puppy killers started to drop, caught off guard. A few dropped before they realized what was happening.

I ran along the edge of the clearing, firing as I did so, but my eyes were on Chambers. She turned and looked back. Even from here, I could see she was surprised. So surprised that she didn't move. An explosion made me duck and her move, but not before giving me a look that would have killed a lesser human. I just smiled and kept moving.

Jersey's bullets had caused one of the trucks to explode and then another one. I spotted a group moving toward him. I pumped the grenade launcher. It gave off a loud thud. A second later, the entire group was engulfed by a fiery blast. I noticed Jersey had ducked behind a tree and was putting in a new magazine. The puppy killers moved forward. I gave him cover, taking out some of them. This caused them to turn. Then Jersey opened up. We caught them in a crossfire, and just like that, it was over. The sound of choppers roaring to life made me whirl around. "NO YOU DON'T!"

I took aim and squeezed. My SCAR clicked empty. It was then that my eyes fell on something beautiful. Tell me there is no God, and he isn't looking out for me. Our packs and weapons were sitting right in front of me.

"Thank you, God! Still not going to church!" I grabbed my hunting rifle and looked over when something whizzed by my head.

Sherman had actually picked up an M16 and was firing at me. I took aim and fired. The ill-dressed man flew back against the chopper, looking very shocked. He dropped to the ground. Chambers was in one of the choppers, twirling her finger. The pilot took this as the signal to lift off. I took aim, but one of the puppy killers jumped into the chopper and blocked my shot. He slumped forward. Both choppers lifted up. Bullets began to hit one of the choppers. Jersey was charging across the clearing, emptying his Tommy gun into it. He was screaming like a madman.

I just had to stop and just admire the man.

The chopper began to smoke and then burn. Then it exploded, dropping to the ground in a flaming heap. The other one lifted up. Jersey ran up, panting like an old man. "She's getting away!"

"Jersey, you know the old saying," I said, taking aim. I sucked in my breath and held it. I moved my scope with the chopper and squeezed two shots. I saw the motor begin to smoke. I put two more into the helicopter just to be sure. Then, tail rotor, just to be sure. I watched the chopper continue to smoke, and then fire came out. It wobbled in the air. Then spun around and around. It seemed to hover for a second before it dropped into the trees. A beautiful billow of fire and smoke rose up. I smiled at my friend. "What goes up must come down."

"We got a jeep," Jersey said, looking over at the jeep.

"Yes, we do."

CHAPTER 40

We didn't bother trying to keep a low cover. I drove the jeep right down into Cornwall and up Main Street. Jersey made some comment about where did I learn to drive? I didn't have the heart to tell him I didn't have a license. I kept meaning to, but I had my bike, and Reggan was always good for a ride. I was surprised at how empty my hometown was. I could see all the businesses were closed. The broken windows told me they had been ransacked and sometimes burned. The snow was piled high, but most of the streets were plowed. This was a good and bad thing. It made travel easy, but it also meant the army kept these streets open for a reason. I parked the jeep about two blocks from Reggan's house. Then Jersey and I hoofed it over, using the snow and trees for cover. We came to her street and stopped.

"I guess they beat us here," Jersey said, staring at the tank parked in front of the house. There were about ten men dressed in green fatigues. These weren't puppy killers but were taking orders from two more men in black. At least these guys were smart enough to wear rubbers over their shoes.

"Reggan!" I snarled when I saw two soldiers carry my friend out and stuff her into the trunk of a car. "Not happening!"

I pulled my rifle off my shoulder and took aim. I got a bead on one of the men in black. I was about to squeeze off the shot when the rifle barrel flew up. I looked over at Jersey in shock. "What the hell are you doing?"

"What are you doing?" Jersey asked, looking at me like I was the crazy person here. "They have a tank!"

"We got grenades. We can take them." I snarled, pushing his hand off my gun and taking aim. Suddenly, his arm went around my neck, and he pushed back. He used his weight to get me flat on my back. I was not going down quietly. He managed to get on top of me, but I still fought him. Didn't he get it? Reggan was right there. We take out these few guys and mission accomplished. "GET OFF ME!"

Jersey clamped his hand over my mouth and leaned in close. He hissed into my face. "Quiet! They will hear you."

I bit his hand. I had to give him credit, but his hand stayed over my mouth. I was really kicking and swinging. Jersey might be tougher than he looked.

"Ellie! This is not the way." He said, his voice almost pleading. He let off another grunt of pain when I got a good kick in his shin. "Listen to me. If you die. Reggan Dies! Everything we have done will be for nothing!"

It was his tone that caught my attention. He was begging me to think. I closed my eyes and tried to relax. My anger slowly faded. I stopped struggling. After a few moments, I nodded. Jersey looked at me and rolled off. He lifted his hand and looked at the bite mark. Then looked at me. "Ow."

I just glared at him, still a little pissed. Then, I crawled back and watched the tank back up. The car with Reggan followed. I gave Jersey my death glare.

"You know something about tanks." He said, still holding his hand. "They are slow and leave a trail even I can follow."

I was still a little annoyed but gave him a snort. We watched the tank turn around. One of the soldiers came out and looked at the men in black. "What do you want to do with the other one?"

"She is not the one we want," one of the guys said. Leave her. We don't even need the other one now."

"I think we should check out the house. See who is in there." Jersey said. "I am pretty sure I know where they are taking her."

"Okay," I muttered, watching them take my friend away. The tank and soldiers quickly followed. We went across the street after we were sure they were gone. The house had been trashed, and some moron had written the word freak on the side. I stepped into the front room. A room that had once been warm and cozy. It was now cold and hard. My eyes took in the wrecked room. There was a dead body on the floor. I walked over and looked down into the face of Thomas Lane. There was a small bullet hole right between his eyes. "Well, Tommy, you have looked better."

"You think he hooked up with Reggan?" Jersey said, joining me by the body. "We got another body."

I looked over at the sofa. A girl was lying on it like she was asleep. She looked familiar. I rushed over and looked down. My whole body went limp, making me drop to the floor. I put my hands on her face and sobbed. "Not you, Trisha. Not you. You didn't hurt anyone."

"She a friend of yours?" Jersey said, keeping his distance.

Trisha was my best friend right after Reggan. Sure, she was a cheerleader, class president, and all that other crap, but she was cool. Like Reggan, I had known her since grade school. Now, she was gone. I pulled her up into my arms and sobbed. As I hugged her close to me, my fingers brushed against something. I pulled it out. It was a dart. It took me a second to realize that she might not be dead. I laid her down and gently patted her face. After a few long moments, she moaned. I laughed. "Jersey! She is alive! She is alive!"

It took a while to wake her up. Jersey was able to make some coffee, which helped. Once Trisha was awake, she began to sob. She kept blubbering on and on about how she had betrayed Reggan and how it was all her fault that Reggan was caught. Then she announced we were going after her.

I had no argument with that.

This was why, an hour later, we were trudging up a path and going up a mountain. The jeep had run out of gas. Jersey had assured us that the base was close by. His hand was nicely bandaged, thanks to me.

I knew this trail, but more importantly, I knew there was a cabin on the other side. It was a small cabin, but it would do. I smiled when the small one-story cabin came into view. It was made of old wood with a massive stone chimney at one end. We stowed our gear. Trisha found a too big jacket, but it was warmer than the one she was wearing. Then she looked at me and asked, as simple as you please, "Which of these guns am I using?"

"The double-barrel shotgun," I said, handing her a box of shells. I opened and closed it. "It's simple. Put the shells in, point, and fire. It is hard to miss with this thing. Be careful; it has a heck of a kick."

"That works," Trisha said, taking the shotgun and shoving shells into her pocket. "Do we have a plan?"

"Let's see what we are up against," I said, checking my MP5 and trusty hunting rifle. "Let's move."

We were just leaving the cabin when a big fat chicken walked right up to me, poked me in the leg, and looked me right in the eye. "Really?"

CHAPTER 41

"I can't believe you killed that chicken," Jersey said, still shaking his head.

"She was asking for it. You saw the look in her eyes, and she poked me in the leg," I said, leading the group down. "A chicken walks up to me and does that. I am thinking of dinner. You will thank me later."

"Not if you're cooking it," Trisha said, moving beside me. "Another reason to save Reggan. We are going to do this. Right?"

"The chicken will be our celebration dinner," I said. "I have come too far now. These jerks are not going to win."

Jersey was right on the money. We came down to the lower hills and looked down at a reasonably big compound. It was just like the one I had escaped from. High barbwire fences with wood towers on the corners. Tents and those half-dome buildings that the army loves. In the middle was a small two-story office building. There were lots of trunks and jeeps. Outside the wire was a small landing field with a couple of choppers. Yes, there were a lot of soldiers. They seemed to be a mix of puppy killers and regular army guys. I used my binoculars to scan the place. I saw one of the men in black standing by the office building. It was one of the guys from Reggan's house. "She is here and in that building. Give me a second."

"Let me see," Trisha said, taking the binoculars. Well, we can't just walk in. Whatever we do will have to wait until the sun sets. Maybe we can cut through the wire. Hello, I got a guy that looks like a general."

I used the scope on my rifle to spot my old buddy Watershaw. I was so tempted to take the shot. It would have been so easy. We were perched on a flat rock that was a perfect sniper's nest. I had a great view of the entire camp. Watershaw walked up to the man in black. They seemed to argue. Then he went into the building. I leaned back.

"It looks like the man in black and the general are not getting along," Trisha said. "I wonder why that is?"

"You have no idea how screwed up the country is right now," Jersey said, giving her a sad smile and shaking his head. "I am losing track of all the players."

"I am not. Watershaw, anyone wearing black and aliens. Bad guys," I said. I pulled out a white cloth that I found at Reggan's house. I wrapped it around the end of my barrel. "Okay, we'll wait until dark. Then you and Trish sneak in. I will watch your backs from up here."

"Not much of a plan," Jersey said, looking down at the camp.

"Works for me," Trisha said, returning the binoculars to her eyes. Do you want to stay up here? That's fine. I will go in. Reggan is in there because of me. I am getting her out."

"I'm not saying we shouldn't go in," Jersey said, looking slightly hurt. "We just need more of a plan."

"There are three of us. That's the plan," I said, looking at Jersey. "Besides, we got the element of surprise on our side."

"Yeah, they will never see us coming," Trisha said, studying the compound. "The fence is real close to the woods on this side. We get through the fence, and we are home free."

"Will you listen to yourselves?" Jersey said. "We are not just going to walk in; grab your friend and walk out. Let's everyone calm down."

"I am calm. Trisha, you calm?"

"I am cool as a cucumber," Trisha said. "Yeah, this is going to work."

"Are you going to let a cheerleader lead the charge?" I asked Jersey.

It was because Trisha was here or we were so close to helping Reggan, but I felt there was nothing better we could do. We were getting Reggan out.

"Please listen to me," Jersey said.

"Guys," Trisha said, her eyes locked on the camp.

"I am listening to you," I said.

"Guys!" Trisha said, still watching the camp.

Jersey and I continued to argue.

"GUYS!"

We both looked at Trisha. She pointed to the camp. "It looks like Reggan is making her own escape."

Jersey and I looked down at the camp. I raised the scope to my eye. Reggan was just outside the building.

Then all hell broke loose.

Alien saucers swooped down from the sky and began firing at the camp. Explosions destroyed the fence. Aliens dressed in green charged into the compound. The army was caught off guard. A lot of guys were taken out. They quickly recovered and returned fire. I was keeping my scope on Reggan. Then, the other side of the compound was attacked. The fence went down. More aliens charged in, but these guys were in blue and using laser guns. I watched in disbelief as the entire compound was turned into a war zone. Reggan was crouching down, looking at something. She started to move in the wrong direction, but explosions forced her back. Some soldiers ran up. He was yelling something and pointing to Reggan. I took aim and squeezed my trigger. Reggan looked surprised but started to move. Two more soldiers came at her, and I took care of them. I was thinking. "Come on Reggan, make your move. I got your back."

"I am going down toward the fence," Trisha said as she moved off.

"I'm going left," Jersey said and ran off.

I just nodded and watched my friend's back. She hooked up with two guys in black and white camo. They had a brief discussion. I took out two aliens. They moved toward the fence. One of them blew up a tanker. I spotted Jersey down by the fence. He took out three soldiers and then tossed three grenades under the fence and ran. The explosions brought down the fence. Reggan and the two soldiers ran for the hole. Three soldiers came out of nowhere. I took them out and watched my friend and the two men run into the woods. "Time to move."

I got up and ran down the hill, jumping over several logs. I pushed through some bushes and stopped. Reggan and the two soldiers were standing under a tree. Everyone was pointing guns at each other. Then

I spotted another man in black. This was all I needed to see. I brought the scope to my eye and fired. One down and then a second. The man in black jumped back. The tree was in my way. I started to move into a better position when Trisha came charging out of the trees like a mad woman.

"That's my girl."

She yelled something and fired both barrels. No more man in black. The blast sent her back onto her butt. I couldn't help but laugh. Then I saw Reggan run over to Trisha and pull her into her arms. They laughed and hugged.

No way was I missing out on this.

I ran down to my two friends and joined the hug fest.

I assume you read Reggan's most excellent book, so I will skip the ending.

I do have to mention Reggan's new eyes. They are so cool. I am so jealous. On top of that, she's got super senses. Some people have all the luck.

CHAPTER 42

I had been sitting by the window listening to Taylor Swift and just being happy. Reggan was asleep on the bed, and Trisha was curled up in front of the fireplace. We had just had a fine meal cooked by Reggan.

Yes, we ate the chicken, and it was delicious.

I noticed Jersey was standing outside. He yawned and then kicked the snow. I turned off my music and went outside. He glanced back and nodded.

"So we found your friend," Jersey said. "Kicked some ass. Now we're going to find Reggan's mom."

"Reggan and I think we should hold up for few days here," I said. "We all need the rest, and yes, we need a plan."

"I'm not going to question your plans anymore," he said, smiling. "Today worked out."

"Jersey," I said, giving him a smile. You should think about going home.

"I am home," he said, holding up his bandaged hand. That really did hurt."

"Go get some rest," I said, shaking my head. It sounded mushy, but there was no way I would shed tears. "I'm too wired to sleep."

"It sounds like the battle is over," he said, moving toward the house. "I wonder who won."

"Does it matter?"

He didn't answer. I turned my music back on and watched the stars. Just as Taylor finished singing about bad blood, a clucking sound came to my ears. I looked around and spotted two chickens coming right toward me. I snorted. Then, they began to poke me in the legs. I looked down. Both looked up with what I took to be a very snotty attitude. Then they poked me again.

"Really?"